W9-ARQ-121

Scribners *Scribners* *Scribners*
Scribners *Scrib* *Scrib*
Scribners *Scribners*
Scribners *Scribners* *Scrib*
Scribners *Scribners* *Scribners*
Scribners *Scribners* *Scrib*
Scribners *Scribners* *Scribners*
Scribners *Scribners* *Scrib*
Scribners *Scribners* *Scribners*
Scribners *Scribners* *Scrib*
Scribners *Scribners* *Scribners*
Scribners *Scribners* *Scrib*
Scribners *Scribners* *Scribners*
Scribners *Scribners* *Scrib*
Scribners *Scribners* *Scribners*
Scribners *Scribners* *Scrib*
Scribners *Scribners* *Scribners*
Scribners *Scribners* *Scrib*
Scribners *Scribners* *Scribners*
Scribners *Scribners* *Scrib*

Scribners

There was no doubt that Faith Usher had a morbid streak. She carried a capsule of cyanide around with her. Just in case.

But was she the sort of girl to doctor her own champagne and die an exhibitionist's death at the annual Grantham House dinner party? Archie Goodwin, on the spot when Faith took that fatal drink, doesn't think so. He reckons that something much more sinister than suicide is involved; something that only his boss, the fat and formidable detective Nero Wolfe can discover.

Wolfe, too caught up with his orchids and his appetite, reckons it's Archie's problem. Until, encouraged on the one hand by a fat cheque, and threatened on the other by four men, he is persuaded that there is indeed a mystery for him to solve.

More than one, as it turns out. And they all revolve around an unlikely combination of philanthropy, deception, blackmail and, of course, murder . . .

The Nero Wolfe Novels

F
STO

REX STOUT
CHAMPAGNE FOR ONE

Scribners

A *Scribners* Book

Copyright © 1952 by Rex Stout

First Edition published in 1959
This edition published in 1992 by arrangement with
Bantam Books, a division of Bantam Doubleday
Dell Publishing Group Inc.

All characters in this publication are fictitious and any resemblance to real persons, living or dead, is purely coincidental.

All rights reserved.
No part of this publication may be reproduced, stored in a retrieval system, or transmitted, in any form or by any means, without the prior permission in writing of the publisher, nor be otherwise circulated in any form of binding or cover other than that in which it is published and without a similar condition including this condition being imposed on the subsequent purchaser.

A CIP cataloue record for this book is available from the British Library

ISBN 0 356 20108 2

Printed in Great Britain by
Mackays of Chatham PLC, Chatham, Kent

Scribners
A Division of
Macdonald & Co (Publishers) Ltd
165 Great Dover Street
London SE1 4YA

A member of Maxwell Macmillan Publishing Corporation

Chapter 1

If it hadn't been raining and blowing that raw Tuesday morning in March I would have been out, walking to the bank to deposit a couple of cheques, when Austin Byne phoned me, and he might have tried somebody else. But more likely not. He would probably have rung again later, so I can't blame all this on the weather. As it was, I was there in the office, oiling the typewriter and the two Marley .38's, for which we had permits, from the same can of oil, when the phone rang and I lifted it and spoke.

'Nero Wolfe's office, Archie Goodwin speaking.'

'Hello there. This is Byne. Dinky Byne.'

There it is in print for you, but it wasn't for me, and I didn't get it. It sounded more like a dying bullfrog than a man.

'Clear your throat,' I suggested, 'or sneeze or something, and try again.'

'That wouldn't help. My tubes are all clogged. Tubes. Clogged. Understand? Dinky Byne – B-Y-N-E.'

'Oh, hallo. I won't ask how you are, hearing how you sound. My sympathy.'

'I need it. I need more than sympathy, too.' It was coming through slightly better. 'I need help. Will you do me a hell of a favour?'

I made a face. 'I might. If I can do it sitting down and it doesn't cost me any teeth.'

'It won't cost you a thing. You know my Aunt Louise. Mrs Robert Robilotti.'

'Only professionally. Mr Wolfe did a job for her once, recovered some jewellery. That is, she hired him and I did the job – and she didn't like me. She resented a remark I made.'

'That won't matter. She forgets remarks. I suppose you know

5

about the dinner party she gives every year on the birthday date of my Uncle Albert, now resting in peace perhaps?'

'Sure. Who doesn't?'

'Well, that's it. Today. Seven o'clock. And I'm to be one of the chevaliers, and listen to me, and I've got some fever. I can't go. She'll be sore as the devil if she has to scout around for a fill-in, and when I phone her I want to tell her she won't have to, that I've already got one. Mr Archie Goodwin. You're a better chevalier than me any day. She knows you, and she has forgotten the remark you made, and anyhow she has resented a hundred remarks I've made, and you'll know exactly how to treat the lady guests. Black tie, seven o'clock, and you know the address. After I phone her, of course she'll ring you to confirm it. And you can do it sitting down, and I'll guarantee nothing will be served that will break your teeth. She has a good cook. My God, I didn't think I could talk so long. How about it, Archie?'

'I'm chewing on it,' I told him. 'You waited long enough.'

'Yeah, I know, but I kept thinking I might be able to make it, until I pried my eyes open this morning. I'll do the same for you some day.'

'You can't. I haven't got a billionaire aunt. I doubt if she has forgotten the remark I made because it was fairly sharp. What if she vetoes me? You'd have to ring me again to call it off, and then ring someone else, and you shouldn't talk that much, and besides, my feelings would be hurt.'

I was merely stalling, partly because I wanted to hear him talk some more. It sounded to me as if his croak had flaws in it. Clogged tubes have no effect on your esses, as in 'seven' and 'sitting', but he was trying to produce one, and he turned 'long' into 'lawd' when it should have been more like 'lawg'. So I was suspecting that the croak was a phoney. If I hadn't had my full share of ego I might also have been curious as to why he had picked on me, since we were not chums, but of course that was no problem. If your ego is in good shape you will pretend you're surprised if a National Chairman calls to tell you his party wants to nominate you for President of the United States, but you're not *really* surprised.

I only stalled him long enough to be satisfied that the croak was a fake before I agreed to take it on. The fact was that the idea appealed to me. It would be a new experience and should increase my knowledge of human nature. It might also be a little ticklish, and even dismal, but it would be interesting to see how they handled it. Not to mention how I would handle it myself. So I told him I would stand by for a call from his Aunt Louise.

It came in less than half an hour. I had finished the oiling job and was putting the guns in their drawer in my desk when the phone rang. A voice I recognized said she was Mrs Robilotti's secretary and Mrs Robilotti wished to speak with me, and I said, 'Is it jewellery again, Miss Fromm?' and she said, 'She will tell you what it is, Mr Goodwin.'

Then another voice, also recognized. 'Mr Goodwin?'

'Speaking.'

'My nephew Austin Byne says he phoned you.'

'I guess he did.'

'You *guess* he did?'

'The voice said it was Byne, but it could have been a seal trying to bark.'

'He has laryngitis. He told you so. Apparently you haven't changed any. He says that he asked you to take his place at dinner at my home this evening, and you said you would if I invited you. Is that correct?'

I admitted it.

'He says that you are acquainted with the nature and significance of the affair.'

'Of course I am. So are fifty million other people – or more.'

'I know. I regret the publicity it has received in the past, but I refuse to abandon it. I owe it to my dear first husband's memory. I am inviting you, Mr Goodwin.'

'Okay. I accept the invitation as a favour to your nephew. Thank you.'

'Very well.' A pause. 'Of course it is not usual, on inviting a dinner guest, to caution him about his conduct, but for this occasion some care is required. You appreciate that?'

'Certainly.'

'Tact and discretion are necessary.'

'I'll bring mine along,' I assured her.

'And of course refinement.'

'I'll borrow some.' I decided she needed a little comfort. 'Don't worry, Mrs Robilotti, I understand the set-up and you can count on me clear through to the coffee and even after. Relax. I am fully briefed. Tact, discretion, refinement, black tie, seven o'clock.'

'Then I'll expect you. Please hold the wire. My secretary will give you the names of those who will be present. It will simplify the introductions if you know them in advance.'

Miss Fromm got on again. 'Mr Goodwin?'

'Still here.'

'You should have paper and pencil.'

'I always have. Shoot.'

'Stop me if I go too fast. There will be twelve at table. Mr and Mrs Robilotti. Miss Celia Grantham and Mr Cecil Grantham. They are Mrs Robilotti's son and daughter by her first husband.'

'Yeah, I know.'

'Miss Helen Yarmis. Miss Ethel Varr. Miss Faith Usher. Am I going too fast?'

I told her no.

'Miss Rose Tuttle. Mr Paul Schuster. Mr Beverly Kent. Mr Edwin Laidlaw. Yourself. That makes twelve. Miss Varr will be on your right and Miss Tuttle will be on your left.'

I thanked her and hung up. Now that I was booked, I wasn't so sure I liked it. It would be interesting, but it might also be a strain on the nerves. However, I was booked, and I rang Byne at the number he had given me and told him he could stay home and gargle. Then I went to Wolfe's desk and wrote on his calendar Mrs Robilotti's name and phone number. He wants to know where to reach me when I'm out, even when we have nothing important on, in case someone yells for help and will pay for it. Then I went to the hall, turned left, and pushed through the swinging door to the kitchen. Fritz was at the big table, spreading anchovy butter on shad roes.

'Cross me off for dinner,' I told him. 'I'm doing my good deed for the year and getting it over with.'

He stopped spreading to look at me. 'That's too bad. Veal birds in casserole. You know, with mushrooms and white wine.'

'I'll miss it. But there may be something edible where I'm going.'

8

'Perhaps a client?'

He was not being nosy. Fritz Brenner does not pry into other people's private affairs, not even mine. But he has a legitimate interest in the welfare of that establishment, of the people who live in that old brownstone on West Thirty-fifth Street, and he merely wanted to know if my dinner engagement was likely to promote it. It took a lot of cash. I had to be paid. He had to be paid. Theodore Horstmann, who spent all his days and sometimes part of his nights with the ten thousand orchids up in the plant rooms, had to be paid. We all had to be fed, and with the kind of grub that Wolfe preferred and provided and Fritz prepared. Not only did the orchids have to be fed, but only that week Wolfe had bought a Coelogyne from Burma for eight hundred bucks, and that was just routine. And so on and on and on, and the only source of current income was people with problems who were able and willing to pay a detective to handle them. Fritz knew we had no case going at the moment, and he was only asking if my dinner date might lead to one.

I shook my head. 'Nope, not a client.' I got on a stool. 'A former client, Mrs Robert Robilotti – someone swiped a million dollars' worth of rings and bracelets from her a couple of years ago and we got them back – and I need some advice. You may not be as great an expert on women as you are on food, but you have had your dealings, as I well know, and I would appreciate some suggestions on how I act this evening.'

He snorted. 'Act with women? You? Ha! With your thousand triumphs! Advice from me? Archie, that is upside down!'

'Thanks for the plug, but these women are special.' With a fingertip I wiped up a speck of anchovy butter that had dropped on the table and licked it off. 'Here's the problem. This Mrs Robilotti's first husband was Albert Grantham, who spent the last ten years of his life doing things with part of the three or four hundred million dollars he had inherited – things to improve the world, including the people in it. I assume you will admit that a girl who has a baby but no husband needs improving.'

Fritz pursed his lips. 'First I would have to see the girl and the baby. They might be charming.'

'It's not a question of charm, or at least it wasn't with Grantham.

9

His dealing with the problem of unmarried mothers wasn't one of his really big operations, but he took a personal interest in it. He would rarely let his name be attached to any of his projects, but he did with that one. The place he built for it up in Dutchess County was called Grantham House and still is. What's that you're putting in?'

'Marjoram. I'm trying it.'

'Don't tell him and see if he spots it. When the improved mothers were graduated from Grantham House they were financed until they got jobs or husbands, and even then they were not forgotten. One way of keeping in touch was started by Grantham himself a few years before he died. Each year on his birthday he had his wife invite four of them to dinner at his home on Fifth Avenue, and also invite, for their dinner partners, four young men. Since his death, five years ago, his wife has kept it up. She says she owes it to his memory – though she is now married to a specimen named Robert Robilotti who has never been in the improving business. Today is Grantham's birthday, and that's where I'm going for dinner. I am one of the four young men.'

'No!' Fritz said.

'Why no?'

'You, Archie?'

'Why not me?'

'It will ruin everything. They will all be back at Grantham House in less than a year.'

'No,' I said sternly. 'I appreciate the compliment, but this is a serious matter and I need advice. Consider: these girls are mothers, but they are improved mothers. They are supposed to be trying to get a toehold on life. Say they are. Inviting them to dinner at that goddam palace, with four young men from the circle that woman moves in as table partners, whom they have never seen before and don't expect ever to see again, is one hell of a note. Okay, I can't help that; I can't improve Grantham, since he's dead, and I would hate to undertake to improve Mrs Robilotti, dead or alive, but I have my personal problem: how do I act? I would welcome suggestions.'

Fritz cocked his head. 'Why do you go?'

'Because a man I know asked me to. That's another question,

why he picked me, but skip it. I guess I agreed to go because I thought it would be fun to watch, but now I realize it may be pretty damn grim. However, I'm stuck, and what's my programme? I can try to make it gay, or clown it, or get one of them talking about the baby, or get lit and the hell with it, or shall I stand up and make a speech about famous mothers like Venus and Mrs Shakespeare and that Roman woman who had twins?'

'Not that. No.'

'Then what?'

'I don't know. Anyway, you are just talking.'

'All right, you talk a while.'

He aimed a knife at me. 'I know you so well, Archie. As well as you know me, maybe. This is just talk and I enjoy it. You need no suggestions. Programme?' He slashed at it with the knife. 'Ha! You will go there and look at them and see, and act as you feel. You always do. If it is too painful you will leave. If one of the girls is enchanting and the men surround her, you will get her aside and tomorrow you will take her to lunch. If you are bored you will eat too much, no matter what the food is like. If you are offended – There's the elevator!' He looked at the clock. 'My God, it's eleven! The larding!' He headed for the refrigerator.

I didn't jump. Wolfe likes to find me in the office when he comes down, and if I'm not there it stirs his blood a little, which is good for him, so I waited until the elevator door opened and his foot-steps came down the hall and on in. I have never understood why he doesn't make more noise walking. You would think that his feet, which are no bigger than mine, would make quite a business of getting along under his seventh of a ton, but they don't. It might be someone half his weight. I gave him enough time to cross to his desk and get himself settled in his custom-built oversize chair, and then went. As I entered he grunted a good morning at me and I returned it. Our good mornings usually come then, since Fritz takes his breakfast to his room on a tray, and he spends the two hours from nine to eleven, every day including Sunday, up in the plant rooms with Theodore and the orchids.

When I was at my desk I announced, 'I didn't deposit the cheques that came yesterday on account of the weather. It may let up before three.'

He was glancing through the mail I had put on his desk. 'Get Dr Vollmer,' he commanded.

The idea of that was that if I let a little thing like a cold gusty March rain keep me from getting cheques to the bank I must be sick. So I coughed. Then I sneezed. 'Nothing doing,' I said firmly. 'He might put me to bed, and in all this bustle and hustle that wouldn't do. It would be too much for you.'

He shot me a glance, nodded to show that he was on but was dropping it, and reached for his desk calendar. That always came second, after the glance at the mail.

'What is this phone number?' he demanded. 'Mrs Robilotti? That woman?'

'Yes, sir. The one who didn't want to pay you twenty grand but did.'

'What does she want now?'

'Me. That's where you can get me this evening from seven o'clock on.'

'Mr Hewitt is coming this evening to bring a Dendrobium and look at the Renanthera. You said you would be here.'

'I know, I expected to, but this is an emergency. She phoned me this morning.'

'I didn't know she was cultivating you, or you her.'

'We're not. I haven't seen her or heard her since she paid that bill. This is special. You may remember that when she hired you and we were discussing her, I mentioned a piece about her I had read in a magazine, about the dinner party she throws every year on her first husband's birthday. With four girls and four men as guests? The girls are unmarried mothers who are being rehabil –'

'I remember, yes. Buffoonery. A burlesque of hospitality. Do you mean you are abetting it?'

'I wouldn't say abetting it. A man I know named Austin Byne phoned and asked me to fill in for him because he's in bed with a cold and can't go. Anyhow, it will give me a fresh outlook. It will harden my nerves. It will broaden my mind.'

His eyes had narrowed. 'Archie.'

'Yes, sir.'

'Do I ever intrude in your private affairs?'

'Yes, sir. Frequently. But you think you don't, so go right ahead.'

'I am not intruding. If it is your whim to lend yourself to that outlandish performance, very well. I merely suggest that you demean yourself. Those creatures are summoned there for an obvious purpose. It is hoped that they, or at least one of them, will meet a man who will be moved to pursue the acquaintance and who will end by legitimating, if not the infant already in being, the future produce of the womb. Therefore your attendance there will be an imposture, and you know it. I begin to doubt if you will ever let a woman plant her foot on your neck, but if you do she will have qualities that would make it impossible for her to share the fate of those forlorn creatures. You will be perpetrating a fraud.'

I was shaking my head. 'No, sir. You've got it wrong. I let you finish just to hear it. If that were the purpose, giving the girls a chance to meet prospects, I would say hooray for Mrs Robilotti, and I wouldn't go. But that's the hell of it, that's not it at all. The men are from her own social circle, the kind that wear black ties six nights a week, and there's not a chance. The idea is that it will buck the girls up, be good for their morale, to spend an evening with the cream and get a taste of caviar and sit on a chair made by Congreve. Of course –'

'Congreve didn't make chairs.'

'I know he didn't, but I needed a name and that one popped in. Of course that's a lot of hooey, but I won't be perpetrating a fraud. And don't be too sure I won't meet my doom. It's a scientific fact that some girls are more beautiful, more spiritual, more fascinating, after they have had a baby. Also it would be an advantage to have the family already started.'

'Pfui. Then you're going.'

'Yes, sir. I've told Fritz I won't be here for dinner.' I left my chair. 'I have to see to something. If you want to answer letters before lunch I'll be down in a couple of minutes.'

I had remembered that Saturday evening at the Flamingo someone had spilled something on the sleeve of my dinner jacket, and I had used cleaner on it when I got home, and hadn't examined it since. Mounting the two flights to my room, I took a look and found it was okay.

Chapter 2

I was well acquainted with the insides of the Grantham mansion, now inhabited by Robilottis, on Fifth Avenue in the Eighties, having been over every inch of it, including the servant's quarters, at the time of the jewellery hunt; and, in the taxi on my way up-town, preparing my mind for the scene of action, I had supposed that the pre-dinner gathering would be on the second floor in what was called the music room. But no. For the mothers, the works.

Hackett, admitting me, did fine. Formerly his manner with me as a hired detective had been absolutely perfect; now that I was an invited guest in uniform he made the switch without batting an eye. I suppose a man working up to butler could be taught all the ins and outs of handling the hat-and-coat problem with different grades of people, but it's so darned tricky that probably it has to be born in him. The way he told me good evening, compared with the way he had formerly greeted me, was a lesson in fine points.

I decided to upset him. When he had my hat and coat I inquired with my nose up, 'How's it go, Mr Hackett?'

It didn't faze him. That man had nerves of iron. He merely said, 'Very well, thank you, Mr Goodwin. Mrs Robilotti is in the drawing-room.'

'You win, Hackett. Congratulations.' I crossed the reception hall, which took ten paces, and passed through the arch.

The drawing-room had a twenty-foot ceiling and could dance fifty couples easily, with an alcove for the orchestra as big as my bedroom. The three crystal chandeliers that had been installed by Albert Grantham's mother were still there, and so were thirty-seven chairs – I had counted them one day – of all shapes and sizes, not made by Congreve, I admit, but not made in Grand Rapids either. Of all the rooms I had seen, and I had seen a lot, that was about the last one I would pick as the place for a quartet of unwed mothers to meet a bunch of strangers and relax. Entering and casting a glance around, I took a walk – it amounted to that – across to where Mrs Robilotti was standing with a group near a portable bar. As I approached she turned to me and offered a hand.

'Mr Goodwin. So nice to see you.'

She didn't handle the switch as perfectly as Hackett had, but it was good enough. After all, I had been imposed on her. Her pale grey eyes, which were set in so far that her brows had sharp angles, didn't light up with welcome, but it was a question whether they ever had lit up for anyone or anything. The angles were not confined to the brows. Whoever had designed her had preferred angles to curves and missed no opportunities, and the passing years, now adding up to close to sixty, had made no alterations. At least they were covered below the chin, since her dress, pale grey like her eyes, had sleeves above the elbows and reached up to the base of her corrugated neck. During the jewellery business I had twice seen her exposed for the evening, and it had been no treat. The only jewellery tonight was a string of pearls and a couple of rings.

I was introduced around and was served a champagne cocktail. The first sip of the cocktail told me something was wrong, and I worked closer to the bar to find out what. Cecil Grantham, the son of the first husband, who was mixing, was committing worse than murder. I saw him. Holding a glass behind and below the bar top, he put in a half-lump of sugar, a drop or two of bitters, and a twist of lemon peel, filled it half full of soda water, set it on the bar, and filled it nearly to the top from a bottle of Cordon Rouge. Killing good champagne with junk like sugar and bitters and lemon peel is of course a common crime, but the soda water was adding horror to homicide. The motive was pure, reducing the voltage to protect the guests of honour, but faced with temptation and given my choice of self-control or soda water in champagne, I set my jaw. I was going to keep an eye on Cecil to see if he did to himself as he was doing to others, but another guest arrived and I had to go to be introduced. He made up the dozen.

By the time our hostess led the way through the arch and up the broad marble stairs to the dining-room on the floor above, I had them sorted out, with names fitted to faces. Of course I had previously met Robilotti and the twins, Cecil and Celia. Paul Schuster was the one with the thin nose and quick dark eyes. Beverly Kent was the one with the long narrow face and big ears. Edwin Laidlaw was the little guy who hadn't combed his hair, or if he had, it refused to oblige.

I had had a sort of an idea that with the girls the best way would be as an older brother who liked sisters and liked to kid them, of course with tact and refinement, and their reactions had been fairly satisfactory. Helen Yarmis, tall and slender, a little too slender, with big brown eyes and a wide curved mouth that would have been a real asset if she had kept the corners up, was on her dignity and apparently had some. Ethel Varr was the one I would have picked for my doom if I had been shopping. She was not a head-turner, but she carried her own head with an air, and she had one of those faces that you keep looking back at because it changes as it moves and catches different angles of light and shade.

I would have picked Faith Usher, not for my doom, but for my sister, because she looked as if she needed a brother more than the others. Actually she was the prettiest one of the bunch, with a dainty little face and greenish flecks in her eyes, and her figure, also dainty, was a very nice job, but she was doing her best to cancel her advantages by letting her shoulders sag and keeping her face muscles so tight she would soon have wrinkles. The right kind of brother could have done wonders with her, but I had no chance to get started during the meal because she was across the table from me, with Beverly Kent on her left and Cecil Grantham on her right.

At my left was Rose Tuttle, who showed no signs of needing a brother at all. She had blue eyes in a round face, a pony tail, and enough curves to make a contribution to Mrs Robilotti and still be well supplied; and she had been born cheerful and it would take more than an accidental baby to smother it. In fact, as I soon learned, it would take more than two of them. With an oyster balanced on her fork, she turned her face to me and asked, 'Goodwin? That's your name?'

'Right. Archie Goodwin.'

'I was wondering,' she said, 'because that woman told me I would sit between Mr Edwin Laidlaw and Mr Austin Byne, but now your name's Goodwin. The other day I was telling a friend of mine about coming here, this party, and she said there ought to be unmarried fathers here too, and you seem to have changed your name – are you an unmarried father?'

Remember the tact, I warned myself. 'I'm half of it,' I told her. 'I'm unmarried. But not, as far as I know, a father. Mr Byne has a cold and couldn't come and asked me to fill in for him. His bad luck and my good luck.'

She ate the oyster, and another one – she ate cheerfully too – and turned again. 'I was telling this friend of mine that if all society men are like the ones that were here the other time, we weren't missing anything, but I guess they're not. Anyway, you're not. I noticed the way you made Helen laugh – Helen Yarmis. I don't think I ever did see her laugh before. I'm going to tell my friend about you if you don't mind.'

'Not at all.' Time out for an oyster. 'But I don't want to mix you up. I'm not society. I'm a working man.'

'Oh!' She nodded. 'That explains it. What kind of work?'

Remember the discretion, I warned myself. Miss Tuttle should not be led to suspect that Mrs Robilotti had got a detective there to keep an eye on the guests of honour. 'You might,' I said, 'call it trouble-shooting. I work for a man named Nero Wolfe. You may have heard of him.'

'I think I have.' The oysters gone, she put her fork down. 'I'm pretty sure . . . Oh, I remember, that murder, that woman, Susan somebody. He's a detective.'

'That's right. I work for him. But I –'

'You too. You're a detective!'

'I am when I'm working, but not this evening. Now I'm playing. I'm just enjoying myself – and I am, too. I was wondering what you meant –'

Hackett and two female assistants were removing the oyster service, but it wasn't that that stopped me. The interruption was from Robert Robilotti, across the table, between Celia Grantham and Helen Yarmis, who was demanding the general ear; and as other voices gave way, Mrs Robilotti raised hers. 'Must you, Robbie? That flea again?'

He smiled at her. From what I had seen of him during the jewellery hunt I had not cottoned to him, smiling or not. I'll try to be fair to him, and I know there is no law against a man having plucked eyebrows and a thin moustache and long polished nails, and my suspicion that he wore a girdle was merely a suspicion, and if he had married Mrs Albert Grantham for her money I freely admit that no man marries without a reason and with her it would have been next to impossible to think up another one, and I concede that he may have had hidden virtues which I had missed. One thing sure, if my name were Robert and I had married a woman fifteen years older than me for a certain reason and she was composed entirely of angles, I would not let her call me Robbie.

I'll say this for him: he didn't let her gag him. What he wanted all ears for was the story about the advertising agency executive who did a research job on the flea, and by gum he stuck to it. I had heard it told better by Saul Panzer, but he got the point in, with only fair audience response. The three society men laughed with tact, discretion, and refinement. Helen Yarmis let the corners of her mouth come up. The Grantham twins exchanged a glance of sympathy. Faith Usher caught Ethel Varr's eye across the table, shook her head, just barely moving it, and dropped her eyes. Then Edwin Laidlaw chipped in with a story about an author who wrote a book in invisible ink, and Beverly Kent followed with one about an army general who forgot which side he was on. We were all one big happy family – well, fairly happy – by the time the squabs were served. Then I had a problem. At Wolfe's table we tackle squabs with our fingers, which is of course the only practical way, but I didn't want to wreck the party. Then Rose Tuttle got her fork on to hers with one hand, and with the other grabbed a leg and yanked, which settled it.

Miss Tuttle had said something that I wanted to go into, tactfully, but she was talking with Edwin Laidlaw, on her left, and I gave Ethel Varr, on my right, a look. Her face was by no means out of surprises. In profile, close up, it was again different, and when it turned and we were eye to eye, once more it was new.

'I hope,' I said, 'you won't mind a personal remark.'

'I'll try not to,' she said. 'I can't promise until I hear it.'

'I'll take a chance. In case you have caught me staring at you I want to explain why.'

'I don't know.' She was smiling. 'Maybe you'd better not. Maybe it would let me down. Maybe I'd rather think you stared just because you wanted to.'

'You can think that too. If I hadn't wanted to I wouldn't have stared. But the idea is, I was trying to catch you looking the same twice. If you turn your head only a little one way or the other it's a different face. I know there are people with faces that do that, but I've never seen one that changes as much as yours. Hasn't anyone ever mentioned it to you?'

She parted her lips, closed them, and turned right away from me. All I could do was turn back to my plate, and I did so, but in a moment she was facing me again. 'You know,' she said, 'I'm only nineteen years old.'

'I was nineteen once,' I assured her. 'Some ways I liked it, and some ways it was terrible.'

'Yes, it is,' she agreed. 'I haven't learned how to take things yet, but I suppose I will. I was silly – just because you said that. I should have just told you yes, someone did mention that to me once. About my face. More than once.'

So I had put my foot in it. How the hell are you going to be tactful when you don't know what is out of bounds and what isn't? Merely having a face that changes isn't going to get a girl a baby. I flopped around. 'Well,' I said, 'I know it was a personal remark, and I only wanted to explain why I had stared at you. I wouldn't have brought it up if I had known there was anything touchy about it. I think you ought to get even. I'm touchy about horses because once I caught my foot in the stirrup when I was getting off, so you might try that. Ask me something about horses and *my* face will change.'

'I suppose you ride in Central Park. Was it in the park?'

'No, it was out West one summer. Go ahead. You're getting warm.'

We stayed on horses until Paul Schuster, on her right, horned in. I couldn't blame him, since he had Mrs Robilotti on his other side. But Edwin Laidlaw still had Rose Tuttle, and it wasn't until the dessert came, cherry pudding topped with whipped cream, that I had a chance to ask her about the remark she had made.

'Something you said,' I told her. 'Maybe I didn't hear it right.'

She swallowed pudding. 'Maybe I didn't say it right. I often don't.' She leaned to me and lowered her voice. 'Is this Mr Laidlaw a friend of yours?'

I shook my head. 'Never saw him before.'

'You haven't missed anything. He publishes books. To look at me, would you think I was dying to know how many books were published last year in America and England and a lot of other countries?'

'No, I wouldn't. I would think you could make out all right without it.'

'I always have. What was it I said wrong?'

'I didn't say you said it wrong. I understood you to say something about the society men that were here the other time, and I wasn't sure I got it. I didn't know whether you meant another party like this one.'

She nodded. 'Yes, that's what I meant. Three years ago. She throws one every year, you know.'

'Yes, I know.'

'This is my second one. This friend of mine I mentioned, she says the only reason I had another baby was to get invited here for some more champagne, but believe me, if I liked champagne so much I could get it a lot quicker and oftener than that, and anyway, I didn't have the faintest idea I would be invited again. How old do you think I am?'

I studied her. 'Oh – twenty-one.'

She was pleased. 'Of course you took off five years to be polite, so you guessed it exactly. I'm twenty-six. So it isn't true that having babies makes a girl look older. Of course, if you had a lot of them, eight or ten, but by that time you would *be* older. I just don't believe I would look younger if I hadn't had two babies. Do you?'

I was on a spot. I had accepted the invitation with my eyes and ears open. I had told my hostess that I was acquainted with the nature and significance of the affair and she could count on me. I had on my shoulders the responsibility of the moral and social position of the community, some of it anyhow, and here this cheerful unmarried mother was resting the whole problem on the single question, had it aged her any? If I merely said no, it hadn't, which would have been both true and tactful, it would imply that I agreed that the one objection to her career was a phoney. To say no and then proceed to list other objections that were not phonies would have been fine if I had been ordained, but I hadn't, and anyway she had certainly heard of them and hadn't been impressed. I worked it out in three seconds, on the basis that while it was none of my business if she kept on having babies, I absolutely wasn't going to encourage her. So I lied to her.

'Yes,' I said.

'What?' She was indignant. 'You do?'

I was firm. 'I do. You admitted that I took you for twenty-six and deducted five years to be polite. If you had had only one baby I might have taken you for twenty-three, and if you had had none I might have taken you for twenty. I can't prove it, but I might. We'd better get on with the pudding. Some of them have finished.'

She turned to it, cheerfully.

Apparently the guests of honour had been briefed on procedure, for when Hackett, on signal, pulled back Mrs Robilotti's chair as she arose, and we chevaliers did likewise for our partners, they joined the hostess as she headed for the door. When they were out we sat down again.

Cecil Grantham blew a breath, a noisy gust, and said, 'The last two hours are the hardest.'

Robilotti said, 'Brandy, Hackett.'

Hackett stopped pouring coffee to look at him. 'The cabinet is locked, sir.'

'I know it is, but you have a key.'

'No, sir, Mrs Robilotti has it.'

It seemed to me that that called for an embarrassed silence, but Cecil Grantham laughed and said, 'Get a hatchet.'

Hackett poured coffee.

Beverly Kent, the one with a long narrow face and big ears, cleared his throat. 'A little deprivation will be good for us, Mr Robilotti. After all, we understood the protocol when we accepted the invitation.'

'Not protocol,' Paul Schuster objected. 'That's not what protocol means. I'm surprised at you, Bev. You'll never be an ambassador if you don't know what protocol is.'

'I never will anyway,' Kent declared. 'I'm thirty years old, eight years out of college, and what am I? An errand boy in the Mission to the United Nations. So I'm a diplomat? But I ought to know what protocol is better than a promising young corporation lawyer. What do you know about it?'

'Not much.' Schuster was sipping coffee. 'Not much *about* it, but I know what it is, and you used it wrong. And you're wrong about me being a promising young corporation lawyer. Lawyers never promise anything. That's about as far as I've got, but I'm a year younger than you, so there's hope.'

'Hope for who?' Cecil Grantham demanded. 'You or the corporations?'

'About that word "protocol",' Edwin Laidlaw said, 'I can settle that for you. Now that I'm a publisher I'm the last word on words. It comes from two Greek words, *prōtos*, meaning "first", and *kolla*, meaning "glue". Now why glue? Because in ancient Greece a *prōtokollon* was the first leaf, containing an account of the manuscript, glued to a roll of papyrus. Today a protocol may be any one of various kinds of documents – an original draft of something, or an account of some proceeding, or a record of an agreement. That seems to support you, Paul, but Bev has a point, because a protocol can also be a set of rules of etiquette. So you're both right. This affair this evening does require a special etiquette.'

'I'm for Paul,' Cecil Grantham declared. 'Locking up the booze doesn't come under etiquette. It comes under tyranny.'

Kent turned to me. 'What about you, Goodwin? I understand you're a detective, so maybe you can detect the answer.'

I put my coffee cup down. 'I'm a little hazy,' I said, 'as to what you're after. If you just want to decide whether you used the word "protocol" right, the best plan would be to get the dictionary. There's one upstairs in the library. But if what you want is brandy, and the cabinet is locked, the best plan would be for one of us to go to a liquor store. There's one at the corner of Eighty-second and Madison. We could toss up.'

'The practical man,' Laidlaw said. 'The man of action.'

'You notice,' Cecil told them, 'that he knows where the dictionary is and where the liquor store is. Detectives know everything.' He turned to me. 'By the way, speaking of detectives, are you here professionally?'

Not caring much for his tone, I raised my brows. 'If I were, what would I say?'

'Why – I suppose you'd say you weren't.'

'And if I weren't what would I say?'

Robert Robilotti let out a snort. '*Touché*, Cece. Try another one.' He pronounced it 'Seese'. Cecil's mother called him 'Sessel', and his sister called him 'Sesse'.

Cecil ignored his father-in-law. 'I was just asking,' he told me. 'I shouldn't ask?'

'Sure, why not? I was just answering.' I moved my head right and left. 'Since the question has been asked, it may be in all your minds. If I were here professionally I would let it stand on my answer to Grantham, but since I'm not, you might as well know it. Austin Byne phoned this morning and asked me to take his place. If any of you are bothered enough you can check with him.'

'I think,' Robilotti said, 'that it is none of our business. I know it is none of my business.'

'Nor mine,' Schuster agreed.

'Oh, forget it,' Cecil snapped. 'What the hell, I was just curious. Shall we join the mothers?'

Robilotti darted a glance at him, not friendly. After all, who was the host? 'I was about to ask,' he said, 'if anyone wants more coffee. No?' He left his chair. 'We will join them in the music room and escort them downstairs and it is understood that each of us will dance first with his dinner partner. If you please, gentlemen?'

I got up and shook my pants legs down.

Chapter 3

I'll be darned if there wasn't a live band in the alcove – piano, sax, two violins, clarinet, and traps. A record player and speaker might have been expected, but for the mothers, spare no expense. Of course, in the matter of expense, the fee for the band was about balanced by the saving on liquids – the soda water in the cocktails, the pink stuff passing for wine at the dinner table, and the brandy ban – so it wasn't too extravagant. The one all-out splurge on liquids came after we had been dancing an hour or so, when Hackett appeared at the bar and began opening champagne, Cordon Rouge, and poured it straight, no dilution or adulteration. With only an hour to go, apparently Mrs Robilotti had decided to take a calculated risk.

As a dancing partner Rose Tuttle was not a bargain. She was equipped for it physically and she had some idea of rhythm, that wasn't it; it was her basic attitude. She danced cheerfully, and of course that was no good. You can't dance cheerfully. Dancing is too important. It can be wild or solemn or gay or lewd or art for art's sake, but it can't be cheerful. For one thing, if you're cheerful you talk too much. Helen Yarmis was better, or would have been if she hadn't been too *damn* solemn. We would work into the rhythm together and get going fine, when all of a sudden she would stiffen up and was just a dummy making motions. She was a good size for me, too, with the top of her head level with my nose, and the closer you get to her wide, curved mouth the better you liked it – when the corners were up.

Robilotti took her for the next one, and a look around showed me that all the guests of honour were taken, and Celia Grantham was heading for me. I stayed put and let her come, and she stopped at arm's length and tilted her head back.

'Well?' she said.

The tact, I figured, was for the mothers, and there was no point in wasting it on the daughter. So I said, 'But is it any better?'

'No,' she said, 'and it never will be. But how are you going to avoid dancing with me?'

'Easy. Say my feet hurt, and take my shoes off.'

She nodded. 'You would, wouldn't you?'

'I could.'

'You really would. Just let me suffer. Will I never be in your arms again? Must I carry my heartache to the grave?'

But I am probably giving a false impression, though I am reporting accurately. I had seen the girl – I say 'girl' in spite of the fact that she was perhaps a couple of years older than Rose Tuttle, who was twice a mother – I had seen her just four times. Three of them had been in that house during the jewellery hunt, and on the third occasion, when I had been alone with her briefly, the conversation had somehow resulted in our making a date to dine and dance at the Flamingo, and we had kept it. It had not turned out well. She was a good dancer, very good, but she was also a good drinker, and along towards midnight she had raised an issue with another lady, and had developed it to a point where we got tossed out. In the next few months she had phoned me off and on, say twenty times, to suggest a rerun, and I had been too busy. For me the Flamingo has the best band in town and I didn't want to get the cold stare for good. As for her persisting, I would like to think that, once she had tasted me, no other flavour would do, but I'm afraid she was just too pigheaded to drop it. I had supposed that she had long since forgotten all about it but here she was again.

'It's not your heart,' I said. 'It's your head. You're too loyal to yourself. We're having a clash of wills, that's all. Besides, I have a hunch that if I took you in my arms and started off with you, after one or two turns you would break loose and take a swing at me and make remarks, and that would spoil the party. I see the look in your eye.'

'The look in my eye is passion. If you don't know passion when you see it you ought to get around more. Have you got a Bible?'

'No, I forgot to bring it. There's one in the library.' From my inside breast pocket I produced my notebook, which is always with me. 'Will this do?'

'Fine. Hold it flat.' I did so and she put her palm on it. 'I swear on my honour that if you dance with me I will be your kitten for better or for worse and will do nothing that will make you wish you hadn't.'

Anyway, Mrs Robilotti, who was dancing with Paul Schuster, was looking at us. Returning the notebook to my pocket, I closed with her daughter, and in three minutes had decided that every allowance should be made for a girl who could dance like that.

The band had stopped for breath, and I had taken Celia to a chair, and was considering whether it would be tactful to have another round with her, when Rose Tuttle approached, unaccompanied, and was at my elbow. Celia spoke to her, woman to woman.

'If you're after Mr Goodwin I don't blame you. He's the only one here that can dance.'

'I'm not after him to dance,' Rose said. 'Anyway I wouldn't have the nerve because I'm no good at it. I just want to tell him something.'

'Go ahead,' I told her.

'It's private.'

Celia laughed. 'That's the way to do it.' She stood up. 'That would have taken me at least a hundred words, and you do it in two.' She moved off towards the bar, where Hackett had appeared and was opening champagne.

'Sit down,' I told Rose.

'Oh, it won't take long.' She stood. 'It's just something I thought you ought to know because you're a detective. I know Mrs Robilotti wouldn't want any trouble, and I was going to tell her, but I thought it might be better to tell you.'

'I'm not here as a detective, Miss Tuttle. As I told you. I'm just here to enjoy myself.'

'I know that; but you *are* a detective, and you can tell Mrs Robilotti if you think you ought to. I don't want to tell her because I know how she is, but if something awful happened and I hadn't told anybody I would think maybe I was to blame.'

'Why should something awful happen?'

She had a hand on my arm. 'I don't say it should, but it might. Faith Usher still carries that poison around, and she has it with her. It's in her bag. But of course you don't know about it.'

'No, I don't. What poison?'

'Her private poison. She told us girls at Grantham House it was cyanide, and she showed it to some of us, in a little bottle. She always had it, in a little pocket she made in her skirt, and she made pockets in her dresses. She said she hadn't made up her mind to kill herself, but she might, and if she did she wanted to have that poison. Some of the girls thought she was just putting on, and one or two of them used to kid her, but I never did. I thought she might really do it, and if she did and I had kidded her I would be to blame. Now she's away from there and she's got a job, and I thought maybe she had got over it, but upstairs a while ago Helen Yarmis was with her in the powder room, and Helen saw the bottle in her bag and asked her if the poison was still in it, and she said yes.'

She stopped. 'And?' I asked.

'And what?' she asked.

'Is that all?'

'I think it's enough. If you knew Faith like I do. Here in this grand house, and the butler, and the men dressed up, and that powder room, and the champagne – this is where she might do it if she ever does.' All of a sudden she was cheerful again. 'So would I,' she declared. 'I would drop the poison in my champagne and get up on a chair with it and hold it high, and call out "Here goes to all our woes" – that's what one of the girls used to say when she drank a Coke – and drink it down, and throw the glass away and get off the chair, and start to sink down to the floor, and the men would rush to catch me – how long would it take me to die?'

'A couple of minutes, or even less if you put enough in.' Her hand was still on my arm and I patted it. 'Okay, you've told me. I'd forget it if I were you. Did you ever see the bottle?'

'Yes, she showed it to me.'

'Did you smell the stuff in it?'

'No, she didn't open it. It had a screw top.'

'Was it glass? Could you see the stuff?'

'No, I think it was some kind of plastic.'

'You say Helen Yarmis saw it in her bag. What kind of a bag?'

'Black leather.' She turned for a look around. 'It's there on a chair. I don't want to point –'

'You've already pointed with your eyes. I see it. Just forget it. I'll see that nothing awful happens. Will you dance?'

She would, and we joined the merry whirl, and when the band paused we went to the bar for champagne. Next I took Faith Usher.

Since Faith Usher had been making her play for a year or more, and the stuff in the plastic bottle might be aspirin or salted peanuts, and even if it were cyanide I didn't agree with Rose Tuttle's notion of the ideal spot for suicide, the chance of anything happening was about one in ten million, but even so, I had had a responsibility wished on me, and I kept an eye both on the bag and on Faith Usher. That was simple when I was dancing with her, since I could forget the bag.

As I said, I would have picked her for my sister because she looked as if she needed a brother, but her being the prettiest one of the bunch may have been a factor. She had perked up some too, with her face muscles relaxed, and, in spite of the fact that she got off the beat now and then, it was a pleasure to dance with her. Also now and then, when she liked something I did, there would be a flash in her eyes with the greenish flecks, and when we finished I wasn't so sure that it was a brother she needed. Maybe cousin would be better.

However, it appeared that she had ideas of her own, if not about brothers and cousins, at least about dancing partners. We were standing at a window when Edwin Laidlaw, the publisher, came up and bowed to her and spoke.

'Will you dance with me, Miss Usher?'

'No,' she said.

'I would be honoured.'

'No.'

Naturally I wondered why. He had only a couple of inches on her in height, and perhaps she liked them taller – me, for instance. Or perhaps it was because he hadn't combed his hair, or if he had it didn't look it. If it was more personal, if he had said something that offended her, it hadn't been at the table, since they hadn't been close enough, but of course it could have been before or after. Laidlaw turned and went, and as the band opened up I was opening my mouth to suggest that we try an encore, when Cecil Grantham came and got her. He was about my height and every hair on his head was in place, so that could have been it. I went and got Ethel Varr and said nothing whatever about her face changing. As we danced I tried not to keep twisting my head around, but I had to maintain surveillance on Faith Usher and her bag, which was still on the chair.

When something awful did happen I hadn't the slightest idea that it was coming. I like to think that I can count on myself for hunches, and often I can, but not that time, and what makes it worse is that I was keeping an eye on Faith Usher as I stood talking with Ethel Varr. If she was about to die, and if I am any damn good at hunches, I might at least have felt myself breathing a little faster, but not even that. I saw her escorted to a chair by Cecil Grantham, fifteen feet away from the chair the bag was on, and saw her sit, and saw him go and return in a couple of minutes with champagne and hand her hers, and saw him raise his glass and say something. I had been keeping her in the corner of my eye, not to be rude to Ethel Varr, but at that point I had both eyes straight at Faith Usher. Not that I am claiming a hunch; it was simply that Rose Tuttle's idea of poison in champagne was fresh in my mind and I was reacting to it. So I had both eyes on Faith Usher when she took a gulp and went stiff, and shook all over, and jerked halfway to her feet, and made a noise that was part scream and part moan, and went down. Going down, she teetered on the edge of the chair for a second and then would have been on the floor if Cecil hadn't grabbed her.

When I got there he was trying to hold her up. I said to let her down, took her shoulders, and called out to get a doctor. As I eased her to the floor she went into convulsion, her head jerking and her legs thrashing, and when Cecil tried to catch her ankles I told him that was no good and asked if someone was getting a doctor, and someone behind me said yes. I was on my knees, trying to keep her from banging her head on the floor, but managed a glance up and around, and saw that Robilotti and Kent and the band leader were keeping the crowd back. Pretty soon the convulsions eased up, and then stopped. She had been breathing fast in heavy gasps, and when they slowed down and weakened, and I felt her neck getting stiff, I knew the paralysis was starting, and no doctor would make it in time to help.

29

Cecil was yapping at me, and there were other voices, and I lifted my head to snap, 'Will everybody please shut up? There's nothing I can do or anyone else.' I saw Rose Tuttle. 'Rose, go and guard that bag. Don't touch it. Stick there and don't take your eyes off it.' Rose moved.

Mrs Robilotti took a step towards me and spoke. 'You are in my house, Mr Goodwin. These people are my guests. What's the matter with her?'

Having smelled the breath of her gasps, I could have been specific, but that could wait until she was dead, not long, so I skipped it and asked, 'Who's getting a doctor?'

'Celia's phoning,' someone said.

Staying on my knees, I turned back to her. A glance at my wristwatch showed me five past eleven. She had been on the floor six minutes. There was foam on her mouth, her eyes were glassy, and her neck was rigid. I stayed put for two minutes, looking at her, ignoring the audience participation, then reached for her hand and pressed hard on the nail of the middle finger. When I removed my fingers the nail stayed white; in thirty seconds there was no sign of returning pink.

I stood up and addressed Robilotti. 'Do I phone the police or do you?'

'The police?' He had trouble getting it out.

'Yes. She's dead. I'd rather stick here, but you must phone at once.'

'No,' Mrs Robilotti said. 'We have sent for a doctor. I give the orders here. I'll phone the police myself when I decide it is necessary.'

I was sore. Of course that was bad; it's always a mistake to get sore in a tough situation, especially at yourself; but I couldn't help it. Not more than half an hour ago I had told Rose to leave it to me, I would see that nothing awful happened, and look. I glanced around. Not a single face, male or female, looked promising. The husband and the son, the two guests of honour, the butler, the three chevaliers – none of them was going to walk over Mrs Robilotti. Celia wasn't there. Rose was guarding the bag. Then I saw the band leader, a guy with broad shoulders and a square jaw, standing at the entrance to the alcove with his back to it, surveying the tableau calmly, and called to him.

'My name's Goodwin. What's yours?'

'Johnson.'

'Do you want to stay here all night, Mr Johnson?'

'No.'

'Neither do I. I think this woman was murdered, and if the police do too you know what that means, so the sooner they get here the better. I'm a licensed private detective and I ought to stay with the body. There's a phone on a stand in the reception hall. The number is Spring seven-three-one-hundred.'

'Right.' He headed for the arch. When Mrs Robilotti commanded him to halt and moved to head him off he just side-stepped her and went on, not bothering to argue, and she called to her men, 'Robbie! Cecil! Stop him!'

When they failed to react she wheeled to me. 'Leave my house!'

'I would love to,' I told her. 'If I did, the cops would soon bring me back. Nobody is going to leave your house for a while.'

Robilotti was there, taking her arm. 'It's no use, Louise. It's horrible, but it's no use. Come and sit down.' He looked at me. 'Why do you think she was murdered? Why do you say that?'

Paul Schuster, the promising young lawyer, spoke up. 'I was going to ask that, Goodwin. She had a bottle of poison in her bag.'

'How do you know she did?'

'One of the guests told me. Miss Varr.'

'One of them told me too. That's why I asked Miss Tuttle to guard the bag. I still think she was murdered, but I'll save my reason for the police. You people might – '

Celia Grantham came running in, calling, 'How is she?' and came on, stopping beside me, looking down at Faith Usher. 'My God,' she said, whispered, and seized my arm and demanded, 'Why don't you *do* something?' She looked down again, her mouth hanging open, and I put my hands on her shoulders and turned her around. 'Thanks,' she said. 'My God, she was so pretty. Is she dead?'

'Yes. Did you get a doctor?'

'Yes, he's coming. I couldn't get ours. I got – What good is a doctor if she's dead?'

'Nobody is dead until a doctor says so. It's a law.' Some of the others were jabbering, and I turned and raised my voice. 'You people might as well rest your legs and there are plenty of chairs, but stay away from the one the bag is on. If you want to leave the room I can't stop you, but I advise you not to. The police might misunderstand it, and you'd only have more questions to answer.' A buzzer sounded and Hackett was going, but I stopped him. 'No, Hackett, you'd better stay, you're one of us now. Mr Johnson will let them in.'

He was doing so. There was no sound of the door opening because doors on mansions do not make noises, but there were voices in the reception hall, and everybody turned to face the arch. In they came, a pair, two precinct men in uniform. They marched in and stopped, and one of them asked, 'Mr Robert Robilotti?'

'I'm Robert Robilotti,' he said.

'This your house? We got –'

'No,' Mrs Robilotti said. 'It's my house.'

Chapter 4

When I mounted the seven steps of the stoop of the old brownstone at twelve minutes after seven Wednesday morning and let myself in, I was so pooped that I was going to drop my topcoat and hat on the hall bench, but breeding told, and I put the coat on a hanger and the hat on a shelf and went to the kitchen.

Fritz, at the refrigerator, turned and actually left the refrigerator door open to stare at me.

'Behold!' he said. He had told me once that he had got that out of his French-English dictionary, many years ago, as a translation of *voilà*.

'I want,' I said, 'a quart of orange juice, a pound of sausage, six eggs, twenty griddle cakes, and a gallon of coffee.'

'No doughnuts with honey?'

'Yes. I forgot to mention them.' I dropped on to the chair I occupy at breakfast, groaning. 'Speaking of honey, if you want to make a friend who will never fail you, you might employ the eggs in a hedgehog omelet, with plenty – No. It would take too long. Just fry 'em.'

'I never fry eggs.' He was stirring a bowl of batter. 'You have had a night?'

'I have. A murder with all the trimmings.'

'Ah! Terrible! A client, then?'

I do not pretend to understand Fritz's attitude towards murder. He deplores it. To him the idea of one human being killing another is insupportable; he has told me so, and he meant it. But he never has the slightest interest in the details, not even who the victim was, or the murderer, and if I try to tell him about any of the fine points it just bores him. Beyond the bare fact that again a human being has done something insupportable, the only question he wants answered is whether we have a client.

'No client,' I told him.

'There may be one, if you were there. Have you had nothing to eat?'

'No. Three hours ago they offered to get me a sandwich at the District Attorney's office, but my stomach said no. It preferred to wait for something that would stay down.' He handed me a glass of orange juice. 'Many, many thanks. That sausage smells marvellous.'

He didn't like to talk or listen when he was actually cooking, even something as simple as broiling sausage, so I picked up the *Times*, there on my table as usual, and gave it a look. A murder has to be more than run-of-the-mill to make the front page of the *Times*, but this one certainly qualified, having occurred at the famous unmarried-mothers party at the home of Mrs Robert Robilotti, and it was there, with a three-column lead on the bottom half of the page, carried over to page 23. But the account didn't amount to much, since it had happened so late, and there were no pictures, not even of me. That settled, I propped the paper on the reading rack and tackled a sausage and griddle cake.

I was arranging two poached eggs on the fourth cake when the house phone buzzed, and I reached for it and said good morning and had Wolfe's voice.

'So you're here. When did you get home?'

'Half an hour ago. I'm eating breakfast. I suppose it was on the seven-thirty newscast.'

'Yes. I just heard it. As you know, I dislike the word "newscast". Must you use it?'

'Correction. Make it the seven-thirty radio news broadcast. I don't feel like arguing, and my cake is getting cold.'

'You will come up when you have finished.'

I said I would. When I had cradled the phone Fritz asked if he was in humour, and I said I didn't know and didn't give a damn. I was still sore at myself.

I took my time with the meal, treating myself to three cups of coffee instead of the usual two, and was taking the last swallow when Fritz returned from taking up the breakfast tray. I put the cup down, got up, had a stretch and a yawn, went to the hall, mounted the flight of stairs in no hurry, turned left, tapped on a door, and was told to come in.

Entering, I blinked. The morning sun was streaking in and glancing off the vast expanse of Wolfe's yellow pyjamas. He was seated at a table by a window, barefooted, working on a bowl of fresh figs with cream. When I was listing the cash requirements of the establishment I might have mentioned that fresh figs in March, by air from Chile, are not hay.

He gave me a look. 'You are dishevelled,' he stated.

'Yes, sir. Also disgruntled. Also disslumbered. Did the broadcast say she was murdered?'

'No. That she died of poison and the police are investigating. Your name was not mentioned. Are you involved?'

'Up to my chin. I had been told by a friend of hers that she had a bottle of cyanide in her bag, and I was keeping an eye on her. We were together in the drawing-room, dancing, all twelve of us, not counting the butler and the band, when a man brought her a glass of champagne, and she took a gulp, and in eight minutes she was dead. It was cyanide, that's established, and the way it works it had to be in the champagne, but she didn't put it there. I was watching her, and I'm the one that says she didn't. Most of the others, maybe all of them, would like to have it that she did. Mrs Robilotti would like to choke me, and some of the others would be glad to lend a hand. A suicide at her party would be bad enough, but a homicide is murder. So I'm involved.'

He swallowed a bite of fig. 'You are indeed. I suppose you considered whether it would be well to reserve your conclusion.'

I appreciated that – his not questioning my eyesight or my faculty of attention. It was a real tribute, and the way I felt, I needed one. I said, 'Sure I considered it. But I had to include that I had been told she had cyanide in her bag, since the girl who told me would certainly include it, and Cramer and Stebbins and Rowcliff would know damn well that in that case I would have had my eyes open, so I had no choice. I couldn't tell them yes, I was watching her and the bag, and yes, I was looking at her when Grantham took her the champagne and she drank it, and yes, she might have put something in the champagne before she drank when I was absolutely certain she hadn't.'

'No,' he agreed. He had finished the figs and taken one of the ramekins of shirred eggs with sausage from the warmer. 'Then you're in for it. I take it that we expect no profitable engagement.'

'We do not. God knows, not from Mrs Robilotti.'

'Very well.' He put a muffin in the toaster. 'You may remember my remarks yesterday.'

'I do. You said I would demean myself. You did not say I would get involved in an unprofitable homicide. I'll deposit the cheques this morning.'

He said I should go to bed, and I said if I did it would take a guided missile to get me up again.

After a shower and shave and tooth brush, and clean shirt and socks, and a walk to the bank and back, I began to think I might last the day out. I had three reasons for making the trip to the bank: first, people die, and if the signer of a cheque dies before the cheque reaches his bank the bank won't pay it; second, I wanted air; and third, I had been told at the District Attorney's office to keep myself constantly available, and I wanted to uphold my constitutional freedom of movement. However, the issue wasn't raised, for when I returned Fritz told me that the only phone call had been from Lon Cohen of the *Gazette*.

Lon has done us various favours over the years, and besides, I like him, so I gave him a ring. What he wanted was an eye-witness story of the last hours of Faith Usher, and I told him I'd think it over and let him know. His offer was five hundred bucks, which would have been not for Nero Wolfe but for me, since my presence at the party had been strictly personal, and of course he pressed – journalists always press – but I stalled him. The bait was attractive, five C's and my picture in the paper, but I would have to include the climax, and if I reported that exactly as it happened, letting the world know that I was the one obstacle to calling it suicide, I would have everybody on my neck from the District Attorney to the butler. I was regretfully deciding that I would have to pass when the phone rang, and I answered it and had Celia Grantham's voice. She wanted to know if I was alone. I told her yes but I wouldn't be in six minutes, when Wolfe would descend from the plant rooms.

'It won't take that long.' Her voice was croaky, but not necessarily from drink. Like all the rest of them, including me, she had done a lot of talking in the past twelve hours. 'Not if you'll answer a question. Will you?'

36

'Ask it.'

'Something you said last night when I wasn't there – when I was phoning for a doctor. My mother says that you said you thought Faith Usher was murdered. Did you?'

'Yes.'

'Why did you say it? That's the question.'

'Because I thought it.'

'Please don't be smart, Archie. Why did you think it?'

'Because I had to. I was forced to by circumstances. If you think I'm dodging, I am. I would like to oblige a girl who dances as well as you do, but I'm not going to answer your question – not now. I'm sorry, but nothing doing.'

'Do you still think she was murdered?'

'Yes.'

'But *why* ?'

I don't hang up on people. I thought I might have to that time, but she finally gave up, just as Wolfe's elevator jolted to a stop at the bottom. He entered, crossed to his chair behind his desk, got his bulk arranged in it to his satisfaction, glanced through the mail, looked at his calendar, and leaned back to read a three-page letter from an orchid-hunter in New Guinea. He was on the third page when the doorbell rang. I got up and stepped to the hall, saw, through the one-way glass panel of the front door, a burly frame and a round red face, and went and opened the door.

'Good Lord,' I said, 'don't you ever sleep?'

'Not much,' he said, crossing the sill.

I got the collar of his coat as he shed it. 'This is an honour, since you must be calling on me. Why not invite me down – Cramer!'

He had headed for the office. My calling him 'Cramer' instead of 'Inspector' was so unexpected that he stopped and about-faced. 'Why,' I demanded, 'don't you ever learn? You know damn well he hates to have anyone march in on him, even you, or especially you, and you only make it harder. Isn't it me you want?'

'Yes, but I want him to hear it.'

'That's obvious, or you would have sent for me instead of coming. If you will kindly –'

Wolfe's bellow came out to us. 'Confound it, come in here!'

Cramer wheeled and went, and I followed. Wolfe's only greeting was a scowl. 'I cannot,' he said coldly, 'read my mail in an uproar.'

Cramer took his usual seat, the red leather chair near the end of Wolfe's desk. 'I came,' he said, 'to see Goodwin, but I –'

'I heard you in the hall. You would enlighten me? That's why you want me present?'

Cramer took a breath. 'The day I try to enlighten you they can send me to the loony house. It's just that I know Goodwin is your man and I want you to understand the situation. I thought the best way would be to discuss it with him with you present. Is that sensible?'

'It may be. I'll know when I hear the discussion.'

Cramer aimed his sharp grey eyes at me. 'I don't intend to go all over it again, Goodwin. I've questioned you twice myself, and I've read your statement. I'm only after one point, the big point. To begin with, I'll tell you something that is not to be repeated. There is not a thing, not a word, in what any of the others have said that rules out suicide. Not a single damn thing. And there's a lot that makes suicide plausible, even probable. I'm saying that if it wasn't for you suicide would be a reasonable assumption, and it seems likely, I only say likely, that that would be the final verdict. You see what that means.'

I nodded. 'Yeah. I'm the fly in the soup. I don't like it any better than you do. Flies don't like being swamped in soup, especially when it's hot.'

He got a cigar from a pocket, rolled it in his palms, put it between his teeth, which were white and even, and removed it. 'I'll start at the beginning,' he said. 'Your being there when it happened. I know what you say, and it's in your statement – the phone call from Austin Byne and the one from Mrs Robilotti. Of course that happened. When you say anything that can be checked it will always check. But did you or Wolfe help it to happen? Knowing Wolfe, and knowing you, I have got to consider the possibility that you wanted to be there, or Wolfe wanted you to, and you made arrangements. Did you?'

I was yawning and had to finish it. 'I beg your pardon. I could just say no, but let's cover it. How and why I was there is fully explained in my statement. Nothing related to it was omitted. Mr Wolfe thought I shouldn't go because I would demean myself.'

'None of the people who were there was or is Wolfe's client?'

'Mrs Robilotti was a couple of years ago. The job was finished in nine days. Except for that, no.'

His eyes went to Wolfe. 'You confirm that?'

'Yes. This is gratuitous, Mr Cramer.'

'With you and Goodwin it's hard to tell what is and what isn't.' He came back to me. 'I'm going to tell you how it stands up to now. First, it was cyanide. That's settled. Second, it was in the champagne. It was in what spilled on the floor when she dropped the glass, and anyway it acts so fast it must have been. Third, a two-ounce plastic bottle in her bag was half full of lumps of sodium cyanide. The laboratory calls them amorphous fragments; I call them lumps. Fourth, she had shown that bottle to various people and told them she wanted to kill herself; she had been doing that for more than a year.'

He shifted in the chair. He always sat so as to have Wolfe head on, but now he was at me. 'Since the bag was on a chair fifteen feet away from her, and the bottle was in it, she couldn't have taken a lump from it when Grantham brought her the champagne, or just before, but she could have taken it any time during the preceding hour or so and had it concealed in her handkerchief. Testing the handkerchief for traces is out because she dropped it and it fell in the spilled champagne – or rather, it's not out but it's no help. So that's the set-up for suicide. Do you see holes in it?'

I killed a yawn. 'Certainly not. It's perfect. I don't say she mightn't have committed suicide, I only say she didn't. As you know, I have good eyes, and she was only twenty feet from me. When she took the champagne from Grantham with her right hand her left hand was on her lap, and she didn't lift it. She took the glass by the stem, and when Grantham raised his glass and said something she raised hers a little higher than her mouth and then lowered it and drank. Are you by any chance hiding an ace? Does Grantham say that when he handed her the glass she dropped something in it before she took hold of it?'

'No. He only says she might have put something in it before she drank; he doesn't know.'

'Well, I do. She didn't.'

'Yeah. You signed your statement.' He pointed the cigar at me.

'Look, Goodwin. You admit there are no holes in the set-up for suicide; how about the set-up for murder? The bag was there on the chair in full view. Did someone walk over and pick it up and open it and take out the bottle and unscrew the cap and shake out a lump and screw the cap back on and put the bottle back in the bag and drop it on the chair and walk away? That must have taken nerve.'

'Nuts. You're stacking the deck. All someone had to do was get the bag – of course I started watching it – and take it to a room that could be locked on the inside – there was one handy – and get a lump and conceal it in his or her handkerchief – thank you for suggesting the handkerchief – and return the bag to the chair. That would take care, but no great nerve, since if he had any reason to think he had been seen taking the bag or returning it he wouldn't use the lump. He might or might not have a chance to use it, anyway.' A yawn got me.

He pointed the cigar again. 'And that's the next point, the chance to use it. The two glasses of champagne that Grantham took were poured by the butler, Hackett; he did all the pouring. One of them had been sitting on the bar for four or five minutes, and Hackett poured the other one just before Grantham came. Who was there, at the bar, during those four or five minutes? We haven't got that completely straight yet, but apparently everybody was, or nearly everybody. You were. By your statement, and Ethel Varr agrees, you and she went there and took two glasses of champagne of the five or six that were there waiting, and then moved off and stood talking, and soon after – you say three minutes – you saw Grantham bring the two glasses to Faith Usher. So you were there. So you might have dropped cyanide in one of the glasses? No. Even granting that you are capable of poisoning somebody's champagne, you would certainly make sure that the right one got it. You wouldn't just drop it in one of the glasses on the bar and walk away, and that applies to all the others, except Edwin Laidlaw, Helen Yarmis, and Mr and Mrs Robilotti. They hadn't walked away. They were there at the bar when Grantham came and got the two glasses. But he took *two* glasses. If one of those four people saw him coming and dropped the cyanide in one of the glasses, you've got to assume that he or she didn't give a damn whether Grantham got it or Faith Usher got it, which is too much for me. But not for you?' He clamped his teeth on the cigar. He never lit one.

'As you tell it,' I conceded, 'I wouldn't buy it. But I have two comments. The first one is that there is one person who did know which glass Faith Usher would get. He handed it to her.'

'Oh? You put it on Grantham?'

'I don't put it on anybody. I merely say that you omitted a detail.'

'Not an important one. If Grantham dropped the poison in at the bar before he picked up the glasses, there were five people right there, and that *did* take nerve. If he dropped it in while he was crossing to Faith Usher it was quite a trick, with a glass in each hand. If he dropped it in after he handed her the glass you would have seen him. What's your second comment?'

'That I have not implied, in my sessions with you and the others, that I have the slightest notion who did it, or how or why. What you have just told me was mostly news to me. My attention was divided between my companion, Ethel Varr, and the bag, and Faith Usher. I didn't know who was at the bar when Grantham came and got the champagne, or who had been there since Hackett poured the glasses that Grantham took. And I still have no notion who did it, or why or how. I only know that Faith Usher put nothing whatever in the champagne before she drank it, and therefore if it was poison in the champagne that killed her she did not commit suicide. That's the one thing I know.'

'And you won't discuss it.'

'I won't? What are we doing?'

'I mean you won't discuss the possibility that you're wrong.'

'That, no. You wouldn't expect me to discuss the possibility that I'm wrong in thinking you're Inspector Cramer, you're Willie Mays.'

He regarded me a long moment with narrowed eyes, then moved to his normal position in the red leather chair, confronting Wolfe. 'I'm going to tell you,' he said, 'exactly what I think.'

Wolfe grunted. 'You often have.'

'I know I have, but I hoped it wouldn't come to this. I hoped Goodwin had realized that it wouldn't do. I think I know what happened. Rose Tuttle told him that Faith Usher had a bottle of cyanide in her bag, and that she was afraid she might use it right there, and Goodwin told her to forget it, that he would see that nothing happened, and from then on he kept surveillance on both Faith Usher and the bag. That is admitted.'

'It is stated.'

'Okay, stated. When he sees her drink champagne and collapse and die, and smells the cyanide, what would his reaction be? You know him and so do I. You know how much he likes himself. He would be hit where it hurts. He would hate it. So, without stopping to consider, he tells them that he thinks she was murdered. When the police come, he knows that what he said will be reported, so he repeats it to them, and then he's committed, and when Sergeant Stebbins and I arrive he repeats it to us. But to us he has to give a reason, so he has one, and a damn good one, and as long as there was a decent possibility that she *was* murdered we gave it full weight. But now – You heard me explain how it is. I was hoping that when he heard me and realized the situation he would see that his best course is to say that maybe he has been a little too positive. That he can't absolutely swear that she didn't put something in the champagne. He has had time to think it over, and he is too intelligent not to see that. That's what I think. I hope you will agree.'

'It's not a question of agreement, it's a question of fact.' Wolfe turned to me. 'Archie?'

'No, sir. Nobody likes me better than I do, but I'm not that far gone.'

'You maintain your position?'

'Yes. He contradicts himself. First he says I acted like a double-breasted sap and then he says I'm intelligent. He can't have his suicide and eat me too. I stand pat.'

Wolfe lifted his shoulders an eighth of an inch, lowered them, and turned to Cramer. 'I'm afraid you're wasting your time, Mr Cramer. And mine.'

I was yawning.

Cramer's red face was getting redder, a sure sign that he had reached the limit of something and was about to cut loose, but a miracle happened: he put on the brake in time. It's a pleasure to see self-control win a tussle. He moved his eyes to me.

'I'm not taking this as final, Goodwin. Think it over. Of course, we're going on with the investigation. If we find anything at all that points to homicide we'll follow it up. You know that. But it's only fair to warn you. If our final definite opinion is that it was suicide, and we say so, and you give your friend Lon Cohen of the *Gazette* a statement for publication saying that you know it was murder, you'll regret it. That, or anything like it. Why in hell it had to be that *you* were there, God only knows. Such a statement from you, as an eye-witness –'

The doorbell rang. I arose, asked Cramer politely to excuse me, stepped to the hall, and through the one-way glass saw a recent social acquaintance, though it took me a second to recognize him because his forty-dollar fedora covered the uncombed hair. I went and opened the door, confronted him, said, 'Ssshhh,' patted my lips with a forefinger, backed up, and beckoned him in. He hesitated, looking slightly startled, then crossed the threshold. I shut the door and, without stopping to relieve him of his hat and coat, opened the door to the front room, which is on the same side of the hall as the office, motioned him in, followed him, and shut the door.

'It's all right here,' I told him. 'Soundproofed, doors and all.'

'All right for what?' Edwin Laidlaw asked.

'For privacy. Unless you came to see Inspector Cramer of Homicide?'

'I don't know what you're talking about. I came to see you.'

'I thought you might have, and I also thought you might prefer not to collide with Cramer. He's in the office chatting with Mr Wolfe, and is about ready to go, so I shunted you in here.'

'I'm glad you did. I've seen all I want of policemen for a while.' He glanced around. 'Can we talk here?'

'Yes, but I must go and see Cramer off. I'll be back soon. Have a chair.'

I went to the door to the hall and opened it, and there was Cramer heading for the front. He didn't even look at me, let alone speak. I thought if he could be rude I could too, so I let him get his own hat and coat and let himself out. When the door had closed behind him I went to the office and crossed to Wolfe's desk. He spoke.

'I will make one remark, Archie. To bedevil Mr Cramer for a purpose is one thing; to do so merely for pastime is another.'

'Yes, sir. I wouldn't dream of it. You're asking me if my position with you, privately, is the same as it was with him. The answer is yes.'

'Very well. Then he's in a pickle.'

'That's too bad. Someone else is too, apparently. Yesterday when I was invited to the party and given the names of the male guests, I wanted to know who they were and phoned Lon Cohen. One of them, Edwin Laidlaw, is a fairly important citizen for a man his age. He used to be pretty loose around town, but three years ago his father died and he inherited ten million dollars, and recently he bought a controlling interest in the Malvin Press, book publishers, and apparently he intends to settle down and –'

'Is this of interest?'

'It may be. He's in the front room. He came to see me, and since my only contact with him was last night it *could* be of interest. I can talk with him there, but I thought I should tell you because you might possibly want to sit in – or stand in. At the hole. In case I need a witness.'

'Pfui.'

'Yeah, I know. I don't want to shove, but we haven't had a case for two weeks.'

He was scowling at me. It wasn't so much that he would have to leave his chair and walk to the hall and on to the alcove, and stand at the hole – after all, that amount of exercise would be good for his appetite – as it was that the very best that could come of it, getting a client, would also be the worst, since he would have to work. He heaved a sigh, not letting it interfere with the scowl, muttered, 'Confound it,' put his palms on the desk rim to push his chair back, and got up and went.

The hole was in the wall, at eye level, eight feet to the right of Wolfe's desk. On the office side it was covered by a picture of a pretty waterfall. On the other side, in a wing of the hall across from the kitchen, it was covered by nothing, and you could not only see through but also hear through. I had once stood there for four solid hours, waiting for someone to appear from the front room to snitch something from my desk. I allowed Wolfe a minute to get himself posted and then went and opened the door to the front room and spoke.

'In here, Laidlaw. It's more comfortable.' I moved one of the yellow chairs around to face my desk.

Chapter 5

Laidlaw sat and looked at me. Three seconds. Six seconds. Evidently he needed priming, so I obliged.

'I thought it was a nice party up to a point, didn't you? Even with the protocol.'

'I can't remember that far back.' He leaned forward. His hair was still perfectly uncombed. 'Look, Goodwin. I want to ask you a straight question, and I hope you'll answer it. I don't see why you shouldn't.'

'I may not either. What?'

'About what you said last night, that you thought that girl was murdered. You said it not only to us, but to the police and the District Attorney. I can tell you confidentially that I have a friend, it doesn't matter who or where, who has given me a little information. I understand that they would be about ready to call it suicide and close the investigation if it weren't for you, so your reason for thinking it was murder must be a pretty good one. That's my question. What is it?'

'Your friend didn't tell you that?'

'No. Either he wouldn't, or he couldn't because he doesn't know. He says he doesn't know.'

I crossed my legs. 'Well, I can't very well say that. So I'll say that I have told only the police and the D.A.'s office and Mr Wolfe, and for the present that's enough.'

'You won't tell me?'

'At the moment, no. Rules of etiquette.'

'Don't you think the people who are involved just because they were there – don't you think they have a right to know?'

'Yes, I do. I think they have a right to demand that the police tell them exactly why they are going ahead with a homicide investigation when everything seems to point to suicide. But they have no right to demand that *I* tell them.'

'I see.' He considered that. 'But the police refuse to tell us.'

'Yeah, I know. I've had experiences with them. I've just had one with Inspector Cramer.'

He regarded me. Four seconds. 'You're in the detective business, Goodwin. People hire you to get information for them, and they pay for it. That's all I want, information, an answer to my question. I'll give you five thousand dollars for it. I have it in my pocket in cash. Of course, I would expect a definitive answer.'

'You would deserve one, for five grand,' I was finding that meeting his eyes halfway, not letting them come on through me, took a little effort. 'Five grand in cash would suit me fine, since the salary Mr Wolfe pays me is far from extravagant. But I'll have to say no even if you double it. This is how it is. When the police make up their minds about it one way or the other, that I'm right or I'm wrong, no matter which, I'll feel free to tell you or anybody else. But if I go spreading it around before then they will say I am interfering with an official investigation, and they will interfere with me. If I lost my licence as a private detective your five grand wouldn't last long.'

'Ten would last longer.'

'Not much.'

'I own a publishing business. I'd give you a job.'

'You'd soon fire me. I'm not a very good speller.'

His eyes were certainly straight and steady. 'Will you tell me this? How good is your reason for thinking it was murder? Is it good enough to keep them on it the whole way, in spite of the influence of a woman in Mrs Robilotti's position?'

I nodded. 'Yes, I'll answer that. It was good enough to bring Inspector Cramer here when he hadn't had much sleep. In my opinion it is good enough to keep them from crossing it off as suicide until they have dug as deep as they can go.'

'I see.' He rubbed his palms together. Then he rubbed them on the chair arms. He had transferred his gaze to a spot on the rug, which was a relief. It was a full minute before he came back to me. 'You say you have told only the police, the District Attorney, and Nero Wolfe. I want to have a talk with Wolfe.'

I raised my brows. 'I don't know.'

'You don't know what?'

'Whether . . .' I let it trail, screwing my lips. 'He doesn't like to mix in when I'm involved personally. Also he's pretty busy. But I'll see.' I arose. 'With him you never can tell.' I moved.

As I turned left in the hall Wolfe appeared at the corner of the wing. He stood there until I had passed and pushed the swing door, and then followed me into the kitchen. When the door had swung shut I spoke.

'I must apologize for that crack about salary. I forgot you were listening.'

He grunted. 'Your memory is excellent and you shouldn't disparage it. What does that man want of me?'

I covered a yawn. 'Search me. If I had had some sleep I might risk a guess, but it's all I can do to get enough oxygen for my lungs so my brain's doing without. Maybe he wants to publish your autobiography. Or maybe he wants you to make a monkey of me by proving it was suicide.'

'I won't see him. You have supplied a reason: that you are involved personally.'

'Yes, sir. I am also involved personally in the income of your detective business. So is Fritz. So is the guy who wrote you that letter from New Guinea, or he'd like to be.'

He growled, as a lion might growl when it realizes it must leave its cosy lair to scout around for a meal. I admit that for him a better comparison would be an elephant, but elephants don't growl. Fritz, at the table shucking clams, started humming a tune, very low, probably pleased at the prospect of a client. Wolfe glared at him, reached for a clam, popped it into his mouth, and chewed. When I pushed the door open and held it, he waited until the clam was down before passing through.

He doesn't like to shake hands with strangers, and when we entered the office and I pronounced names he merely gave Laidlaw a nod en route to his desk. Before I went to mine I asked Laidlaw to move to the red leather chair so I wouldn't have him in profile as he faced Wolfe. As I sat, Laidlaw was saying that he supposed Goodwin had told Wolfe who he was, and Wolfe was saying yes, he had.

Laidlaw's straight, steady eyes were now at Wolfe instead of me.

'I want,' he said, 'to engage you professionally. Do you prefer the retainer in cash, or a cheque?'

Wolfe shook his head. 'Neither, until I accept the engagement. What do you want done?'

'I want you to get some information for me. You know what happened at Mrs Robilotti's house last evening. You know that a girl named Faith Usher was poisoned and died. You know of the circumstances indicating that she committed suicide. Don't you?'

Wolfe said yes.

'Do you know that the authorities have not accepted it as a fact that she killed herself? That they are continuing with the investigation on the assumption that she might have been murdered?'

Wolfe said yes.

'Then it's obvious that they must have knowledge of some circumstance other than the ones I know about – or that any of us know about. They must have some reason for not accepting the fact that it was suicide. I don't know what that reason is, and they won't tell me, and as one of the people involved – involved simply because I was there – I have a legitimate right to know. That's the information I want you to get for me. I'll give you a retainer now, and your bill can be any amount you think is fair, and I'll pay it.'

I was not yawning. I must say I admired his gall. Though he didn't know that Wolfe had been at the hole, he must have assumed that I had reported the offer he had made, and here he was looking Wolfe straight in the eye, engaging him professionally, and telling him he could name his figure, no matter what, whereas with me ten grand had been his limit. The gall of the guy! I had to admire him.

The corners of Wolfe's mouth were up. 'Indeed,' he said. Laidlaw took a breath, but it came out merely as used air, not as words.

'Mr Goodwin has told me,' Wolfe said, 'of the proposal you made to him. I am at a loss whether to respect your doggedness and applaud your dexterity or to deplore your naïveté. In any case I must decline the engagement. I already have the information you're after, but I got it from Mr Goodwin in confidence and may not disclose it. I'm sorry, sir.'

Laidlaw took another breath. 'I'm not as dogged as you are,' he declared. 'Both of you. In the name of God, what's so top secret about it? What are you afraid of?'

Wolfe shook his head. 'Not afraid, Mr Laidlaw, merely discreet. When a matter in which we have an interest and a commitment requires us to nettle the police we are not at all reluctant. In this affair Mr Goodwin is involved solely because he happened to be there, just as you are, and I am not involved at all. It is not a question of fear or of animus. I am merely detached. I will not, for instance, tell the police of the offers you have made Mr Goodwin and me because it would stimulate their curiosity about you, and since I assume you have made the offers in good faith I am not disposed to do you an ill turn.'

'But you're turning me down.'

'Yes. Flatly. In the circumstances I have no choice. Mr Goodwin can speak for himself.'

Laidlaw's head turned to me and I had the eyes again. I wouldn't have put it past him to renew his offer, with an amendment that he would now leave the figure up to me, but if he had that in mind he abandoned it when he saw my steadfast countenance. When, after regarding me for eight seconds, he left his chair, I thought he was leaving the field and Wolfe wouldn't have to go to work after all, but no. He only wanted to mull, and preferred to have his face to himself. He asked, 'May I have a minute?' and, when Wolfe said yes, he turned his back and moseyed across the rug towards the far wall, where the big globe stood in front of bookshelves; and, for double the time he had asked for, at least that, he stood revolving the globe. Finally he about-faced and returned to the red leather chair, not moseying.

'I must speak with you privately,' he told Wolfe.

'You are,' Wolfe said snortly. 'If you mean alone, no. If a confidence weren't as safe with Mr Goodwin as with me he wouldn't be here. His ears are mine, and mine are his.'

'This isn't only a confidence. I'm going to tell you something that no one on earth knows about but me. I'm going to risk telling you because I have to, but I'm not going to double the risk.'

'You will not be doubling it.' Wolfe was patient. 'If Mr Goodwin left us I would give him a signal to listen to us on a contraption in another room, so he might as well stay.'

'You don't make it any easier, Wolfe.'

'I don't pretend to make things easier. I only make them manageable – when I can.'

Laidlaw looked as if he needed to mull some more, but he got it decided without going to consult the globe again. 'You'll have all you can do to manage this,' he declared. 'I couldn't go to my lawyer with it, or anyhow I wouldn't, and even if I had it would have been too much for him. I thought I couldn't go to anybody, and then I thought of you. You have the reputation of a wizard, and God knows I need one. First I wanted to know why Goodwin thinks it was murder, but evidently you're not going – by the way –'

He took a pen from a pocket and a chequebook from another, put the book on the little table at his elbow, and wrote. He yanked the cheque off, glanced it over, got up to put it on Wolfe's desk, and returned to the chair.

'If twenty thousand isn't enough,' he said, 'for a retainer and advances for expenses, say so. You haven't accepted the job, I know, but I'm camping here until you do. You spoke of managing things. I want you to manage that if they go on with their investigation it doesn't go deep enough to uncover and make public a certain event in my life. I also want you to manage that I don't get arrested and put on trial for murder.'

Wolfe grunted. 'I could give no guarantee against either contingency.'

'I don't expect you to. I don't expect you to pass miracles, either. And two things I want to make plain: first, if Faith Usher was murdered I didn't kill her and don't know who did; and second, my own conviction is that she committed suicide. I don't know what Goodwin's reason is for thinking she was murdered, but whatever it is, I'm convinced that he's wrong.'

Wolfe grunted again. 'Then why come to me in a dither? If you're convinced it was suicide. Since they are human the police do frequently fumble, but usually they arrive at the truth. Finally.'

'That's the trouble. Finally. This time, before they arrive, they might run across the event I spoke of, and if they do, they might charge me with murder. Not they might, they would.'

'Indeed. It must have been an extraordinary event. If that is what you intend to confide in me, I make two remarks: that you are not yet my client, and that even if you were, disclosures to a private detective by a client are not a privileged communication. It's an impasse, Mr Laidlaw. I can't decide whether to accept your job until I know what the event was; but I will add that if I do accept it I will go far to protect the interest of a client.'

'I'm desperate, Wolfe,' Laidlaw said. He pushed his hair back, but it needed more than a push. 'I admit it. I'm desperate. You'll accept the job because there's no reason why you shouldn't. What I'm going to tell you is known to no one on earth but me, I'm pretty sure of that, but not absolutely sure, and that's the devil of it.'

He pushed at his hair again. 'I'm not proud of this, what I'm telling you. I'm thirty-one years old. In August, nineteen fifty-six, a year and a half ago, I went into Cordoni's on Madison Avenue to buy some flowers, and the girl who waited on me was attractive, and that evening I drove her to a place in the country for dinner. Her name was Faith Usher. Her vacation was to start in ten days, and by the time it started I had persuaded her to spend it in Canada with me. I didn't use my own name; I'm almost certain she never knew what it was. She only had a week, and when we got back she went back to work at Cordoni's, and I went to Europe and was gone two months. When I returned I had no idea of resuming any relations with her, but I had no reason to avoid her, and I stopped in at Cordoni's one day. She was there, but she would barely speak to me. She asked me, if I came to Cordoni's again, to get someone else to wait on me.'

'I suggest,' Wolfe put in, 'that you confine this to the essentials.'

'I am. I want you to know just how it was. I don't like to feel that I owe anyone anything, especially a woman, and I phoned her twice to get her to meet me and have a talk, but she wouldn't. So I dropped it. I also stopped buying flowers at Cordoni's, but some months later, one rainy day in April, I went there because it was convenient, and she wasn't there. I didn't ask about her. I include these details because you ought to know what the chances are that the police are going to dig this up.'

'First the essentials,' Wolfe muttered.

'All right, but you ought to know how I found out that she was at Grantham House. Grantham House is an institution started by –'

'I know what it is.'

'Then I don't have to explain it. A few days after I had noticed that she wasn't at Cordoni's a friend of mine told me – his name is Austin Byne, and he is Mrs Robilotti's nephew – he told me that he had been at Grantham House the day before on an errand for Mrs Robilotti and had seen a girl there that he recognized. He said I might recognize her too – the girl with the little oval face and green eyes who used to work at Cordoni's. I told him I doubted it, that I didn't remember her. But I –'

'Was Mr Byne's tone or manner suggestive?'

'No. I didn't think – I'm sure it wasn't. But I wondered. Naturally. It had been eight months since the trip to Canada, and I did not believe that she had been promiscuous. I decided that I must see her and talk with her. I prefer to think that my chief reason was my feeling of obligation, but I don't deny that I also wanted to know if she had found out who I was, and if so whether she had told anyone or was going to. In arranging to see her I took every possible precaution. Shall I tell you exactly how I managed it?'

'Later, perhaps.'

'All right, I saw her. She said that she had agreed to meet me only because she wanted to tell me that she never wanted to see me or hear from me again. She said she didn't hate me – I don't think she was capable of hate – but that I meant only one thing to her, a mistake that she would never forgive herself for, and that she only wanted to blot me out. Those were her words: "blot you out". She said her baby would be given for adoption and would never know who its parents were. I had money with me, a lot of it, but she wouldn't take a cent. I didn't raise the question whether there could be any doubt that I was the father. You wouldn't either, if it had been you, with her, the way she was.'

He stopped and set his jaw. After a moment he released it. 'That was when I decided to quit playing around. I made an anonymous contribution to Grantham House. I never saw her again until last night. I didn't kill her. I am convinced she killed herself, and I hope to God my being there, seeing me again, wasn't what made her do it.'

He stopped again. Then he went on, 'I didn't kill her, but you can see where I'll be if the police go on investigating and dig this up somehow – though I don't know how. They would have me. I was standing at the bar when Cecil Grantham came and got the champagne and took it to her. Even if I wasn't convicted of murder, even if I was never put on trial, this would all come out and that would be nearly as bad. And evidently, if it weren't for Goodwin, for what he has told them, they would almost certainly call it suicide and close it. Can you wonder that I want to know what he told them? At any price?'

'No,' Wolfe conceded. 'Accepting your account as candid, no. But you have shifted your ground. You wanted to hire me to tell you what Mr Goodwin has told the police, though you didn't put it that way, and I declined. What do you want to hire me to do now?'

'To manage this for me. You said you manage things. To manage that this is not dug up, that my connection with Faith Usher does not become known, that I am not suspected of killing her.'

'You're already suspected. You were there.'

'That's nonsense. You're quibbling. I wouldn't be suspected if it weren't for Goodwin. Nobody would be.'

I permitted myself an inside grin. 'Quibble' was one of Wolfe's pet words. Dozens of people, sitting in the red leather chair, had been told by him that they were quibbling, and now he was getting it back, and he didn't like it.

He said testily, 'But you *are* suspected, and you'd be a ninny to hire me to prevent something that has already happened. You have admitted you're desperate, and desperate men can't think straight, so I should make allowances, and I do. That the police will not discover your connection with Faith Usher is a forlorn hope. Surely she knew your real name. Weren't you known at Cordoni's? Didn't you have a charge account?'

'No. I have charge accounts, of course, but not at any florist's. I always paid cash for flowers – in those days. Now it doesn't matter, but then it was more – uh – it was wiser. I don't think she ever knew my name, and even if she did I'm almost certain she never told anyone about me – about the trip to Canada.'

Wolfe was sceptical. 'Even so,' he grumbled. 'You appeared with her in public places. On the street. You took her to dinner. If the police persist it's highly probable that they'll turn it up; at that sort of thing they're extremely proficient. The only way to ward that off with any assurance would be to arrange that they do not persist, and that rests with Mr Goodwin.' His head turned. 'Archie. Has anything that Mr Laidlaw has said persuaded you that you might have been mistaken?'

'No,' I said. 'Now that we can name the figure I admit it's a temptation, but I'm committed. No.'

'Committed to *what*?' Laidlaw demanded.

'To my statement that Faith Usher didn't kill herself.'

'Why? For God's sake, *why*?'

Wolfe took over. 'No, sir. That is still reserved, even if I accept your retainer. If I do, I'll proceed on the hypothesis that your account of your relations with Faith Usher is bona fide, but only as a hypothesis. Over the years I have found many hypotheses untenable. It is quite possible that you did kill Faith Usher and your coming to me is a step in some devious and crafty stratagem. Then –'

'I didn't.'

'Very well. That's an item of the hypothesis. Then the situation is this: since Mr Goodwin is unyielding, and since if the police persist they will surely bare your secret and then harass you, I can do your job only (a) by proving that Faith Usher committed suicide and Mr Goodwin is wrong, or (b) by identifying and exposing the murderer. That would be a laborious and expensive undertaking, and I'll ask you to sign a memorandum stating that, no matter who the murderer is, if I expose him you'll pay my bill.'

Laidlaw didn't hesitate. 'I'll sign it.'

'With, as I said, no guarantee.'

'As I said, I don't expect any.'

'Then that's understood.' Wolfe reached to pick up the cheque. 'Archie. You may deposit this as a retainer and advance for expenses.'

I got up and took it and dropped it in a drawer of my desk.

'I want to ask a question,' Laidlaw said. He was looking at me. 'Evidently you didn't tell the police what happened when I asked

Faith Usher to dance with me, and she refused. If you had told them they would certainly have asked me about it. Why didn't you?'

I sat down. 'That's about the only thing I left out. For a reason. From the beginning they were on my neck about my thinking it was murder, and if I had told them about her refusing to dance with you they would have thought I was also trying to pick the murderer, and they already had certain feelings about me on account of former collisions. And if you denied it when they asked you about it, they might think I was playing hopscotch. I could always remember it and report it later, if developments called for it.'

Wolfe was frowning. 'You didn't report this to me.'

'No, sir. Why should I? You weren't interested.'

'I am now. But now, conveniently, her refusal is already explained.' He turned to the client. 'Did you know Miss Usher would be there before you went?'

'No,' Laidlaw said. 'If I had I wouldn't have gone.'

'Did she know you would be there?'

'I don't know, but I doubt it. I think that goes for her too; if she had she wouldn't have gone.'

'Then it was a remarkable coincidence. In a world that operates largely at random, coincidences are to be expected, but any one of them must always be mistrusted. Had you attended any of those affairs previously? Those annual dinners?'

'No. It was on account of Faith Usher that I accepted the invitation. Not to see her – as I said, I wouldn't have gone if I had known she would be there – just some feeling about what had happened. I suppose a psychiatrist would call it a feeling of guilt.'

'Who invited you?'

'Mrs Robilotti.'

'Were you a frequent guest at her house?'

'Not frequent, no, just occasional. I have known Cecil, her son, since prep school, but we have never been close. Her nephew, Austin Byne, was in my class at Harvard. What are you doing, investigating me?'

Wolfe didn't reply. He glanced up at the wall clock: ten minutes past one. He took in a couple of bushels of air through his nose,

56

and let it out through his mouth. He looked at the client, not with enthusiasm.

'This will take hours, Mr Laidlaw. Just to get started with you – what you know about those people – since I must proceed, tentatively, on the hypothesis that Mr Goodwin is right and Miss Usher was murdered, and you didn't kill her, and therefore one of the others did. Eleven of them, if we include the butler – no, ten, since I shall arbitrarily eliminate Mr Goodwin. Confound it, an army! It's time for lunch, and I invite you to join us, and then we'll resume. Clams hashed with eggs, parsley, green peppers, chives, fresh mushrooms, and sherry. Mr Goodwin drinks milk. I drink beer. Would you prefer white wine?'

Laidlaw said yes, he would, and Wolfe got up and headed for the kitchen.

Chapter 6

At a quarter past five that afternoon, when Laidlaw left, I had thirty-two pages of shorthand, my private brand, in my book. Of course, Wolfe had gone up to the plant rooms at four o'clock so for the last hour and a quarter I had been the emcee. When Wolfe came down to the office at six I had typed four pages from my notes and was banging away on the fifth.

Most of it was a waste of time and paper, but there were items that might come in handy. To begin with, there was nothing whatever on the three unmarried mothers who were still alive. Laidlaw had never seen or heard of Helen Yarmis or Ethel Varr or Rose Tuttle before the party. Another blank was Hackett. All I had got on him was that he was a good butler, which I already knew, and that he had been there for years, since before Grantham had died.

Mrs Robilotti. Laidlaw didn't care much for her. He didn't put it that way, but it was obvious. He called her a vulgarian. Her first husband, Albert Grantham, had had genuine philanthropic impulses and knew what to do with them, but she was a phoney. She wasn't actually continuing to support his philanthropies; they had been provided for in his will; she spent a lot of time on them, attending board meetings and so on, only to preserve her standing with her betters. 'Betters,' for Laidlaw, evidently didn't mean people with more money, which I thought was a broad-minded attitude for a man with ten million of his own.

Robert Robilotti. Laidlaw cared for him even less, and said so. Mrs Albert Grantham, widow, had acquired him in Italy and brought him back with her luggage. That alone showed she was a vulgarian, but here, it seemed to me, things got confused, because Robilotti was not a vulgarian. He was polished, civilized, and well informed. In all this I'm merely quoting Laidlaw. Of course, he was also a parasite. When I asked if he looked elsewhere for the female refreshments that were in short supply at home, Laidlaw said there were rumours, but there were always rumours.

Celia Grantham. Here I had got a surprise – nothing startling, but enough to make me lift a brow. Laidlaw had asked her to marry him six months ago and she had refused. 'I tell you that,' he said, 'so you will know that I can't be very objective about her. Perhaps I was lucky. That was when I was getting a hold on myself after what had happened with Faith Usher, and perhaps I was just looking for help. Celia could help a man all right if she wanted to. She has character, but she hasn't decided what to do with it. The reason she gave for refusing to marry me was that I didn't dance well enough.' It was while we were on Celia that I learned that Laidlaw had an old-fashioned streak. When I asked him what about her relations with men and got a vague answer, and made it more specific by asking if he thought she was a virgin, he said of course, since he had asked her to marry him. An old fogy at thirty-one.

Cecil Grantham. On him it struck me that Laidlaw was being diplomatic, and I thought I guessed why. Cecil was three years younger than Laidlaw, and I gathered that his interests and activities were along the same lines as Laidlaw's had been three years ago before the event with Faith Usher had pushed his nose in – with qualifications, one being that whereas Laidlaw's pile had been left to him with no strings attached, Cecil's was in a trust controlled by his mother and he had to watch his budget. He had been heard to remark that he would like to do something to earn some money but couldn't find any spare time for it. Each year he spent three summer months on a ranch in Montana.

Paul Schuster. He was a prodigy. He had worked his way through college and law school, and when he had graduated with high honours a clerkship had been offered him by a justice of the United States Supreme Court, but he had preferred to go to work for a Wall Street firm with five names at the top, and a dozen at the side, of its letterhead. Probably a hundred and twenty bucks a week. Even more probably, at fifty he would be raking in half a million a year. Laidlaw knew him only fairly well and could furnish no information about the nature and extent of his intimacies with either sex. The owner of one of the five names at the top of the letterhead, now venerable, had been Albert Grantham's lawyer, and that was probably the connection that had got Schuster at Mrs Robilotti's dinner table.

Beverly Kent. Of the Rhode Island Kents, if that means anything to you. It didn't to me. His family was still hanging on to three thousand acres and a couple of miles of a river named Usquepaugh. He too had been in Laidlaw's class at Harvard, and had followed a family tradition when he chose the diplomatic service for a career. In Laidlaw's opinion it wasn't likely that he had ever been guilty of an indiscretion, let alone an outrage, with a female.

Edwin Laidlaw. A reformed man, a repentant sinner, and a recovered soul. He said he had more appropriate clichés handy, but I told him those would do. When he had inherited his father's stack, three years ago, he had gone on as before, horsing around, and had caught up with himself only after the Faith Usher affair. He had not, to the best of his knowledge, ever made any other woman a mother, married or unmarried. It had taken more than half of his assets to buy the Malvin Press, and for four months he had been spending ten hours a day at his office, five days a week, not to mention evenings and weekends. He thought he would be on to the publishing business in five years.

As for Faith Usher, his thinking that she had not been promiscuous, and his not raising the question, at his last meeting with her, whether there was any doubt about his being the father of the baby she was carrying, had been based entirely on the impression he had got of her. He knew nothing whatever about her family or background. He hadn't even known where she lived; she had refused to tell him. She had given him a phone number and he had called her at it, but he didn't remember what it was, and he had made a little private ceremony of destroying his phone-number book when he had reformed. When I said that on a week's vacation trip there is time for a lot of talk, he said they had done plenty of talking, but she had shied away from anything about her. His guess was that she had probably graduated from high school.

We had spent a solid hour with him on the party before Wolfe went up to the plant rooms. Wolfe took him through every minute of it, trying to get some faint glimmer of a hint. Laidlaw was sure that neither he nor Faith Usher had said or done anything that could have made anyone suspect they had ever met before, except her refusing to dance with him, and no one had heard that but me. He had asked her to dance because he thought it would be noticed if he didn't.

Of course the main point was when Cecil Grantham came to the bar to get the champagne. Laidlaw had been standing there with Helen Yarmis, with whom he had just been dancing, and Mr and Mrs Robilotti. As he and Helen Yarmis approached the bar, Beverly Kent and Celia Grantham were moving away, and Mr and Mrs Robilotti were there, and of course Hackett. Laidlaw thought he and Helen Yarmis had been there more than a minute, but not more than two, when Cecil Grantham came; that was what he had told the police. He couldn't say whether, when he had taken two glasses of champagne for Helen Yarmis and himself, there had been other glasses on the bar with champagne in them; he simply hadn't noticed. The police had got him to try to recall the picture, but he couldn't. All he was sure of was that he hadn't poisoned any champagne, but he was almost as sure that Helen Yarmis hadn't either. She had been right at his elbow.

There was more, a lot more, but that's enough for here. You can see why I said that most of it was a waste of time and paper. I might mention that Wolfe had dictated the memorandum, and I had typed it, and Laidlaw had signed it. Also, as instructed by Wolfe, as soon as Laidlaw had gone I phoned Saul Panzer, Fred Durkin, and Orrie Cather, and asked them to drop in at nine o'clock.

At six, on the dot as always, Wolfe entered and crossed to his desk. I collated the originals of the four finished pages, took them to him, and went back to the typewriter. I was rolling out the fifth page when he spoke.

'Archie.'

I twisted my neck. 'Yes, sir?'

'Your attention, please.'

I swivelled. 'Yes, sir.'

'You will agree that this is a devil of a problem, with monstrous difficulties in a disagreeable context.'

'Yes, sir.'

'I have asked you three times regarding your contention that Miss Usher did not commit suicide. The first time it was merely civil curiosity. The second time, in the presence of Mr Cramer, it was merely rhetorical, to give you an opportunity to voice your resolution. The third time, in the presence of Mr Laidlaw, it was merely by the way, since I knew you wouldn't pull back with him here. Now I ask you again. You know how it stands. If I undertake this job, on the assumption that she was murdered, an assumption based solely on your testimony, you know what it will entail in time, energy, wit, and vexation. The expense will be on Mr Laidlaw, but the rest will be on me. I don't care to risk, in addition, the chance that I am burrowing in an empty hole. So I ask you again.'

I nodded. 'I knew this would come. Naturally. I stand pat. I can make a speech if you want one.'

'No. You have already explained your ground. I will only remind you that the circumstances as described by Mr Cramer indicate that it would have been impossible for anyone to poison that glass of champagne with any assurance that it would get to Miss Usher.'

'I heard him.'

'Yes. There is the same objection to supposing that it was intended for any other particular person, and its getting to Miss Usher was a mishap.'

'Right.'

'There is also the fact that she was the most likely target, since the poison was in her bag, making it highly probable that the conclusion would be that she had killed herself. But for you, that would be the conclusion. Therefore it was almost certainly intended for her.'

'Right.'

'But, for the reasons given by Mr Cramer, it couldn't possibly have been intended for her.'

I grinned at him. 'What the hell,' I said. 'I know it's a lulu. I admit I wouldn't know where to start, but I'm not supposed to. That's your part. Speaking of starting, Saul and Fred and Orrie will be here at nine o'clock.'

He made a face. He had to cook up chores for them, nine o'clock was less than three hours away, for one of the hours he would be dining, and he would not work his brain at the table.

'I have,' he growled, 'only this moment committed myself, after consulting you. Mr Laidlaw's cheque could have been returned.' He flattened his palms on the chair arms. 'Then I'm in for it, and so are you. You will go tomorrow morning to that institution, Grantham House, and learn about Faith Usher. How she got there, when she came and when she left, what happened to her infant – everything. Cover it.'

'I will if I can get in. I mention as a fact, not an objection, that that place has certainly had a lot of visitors today. At least a dozen assorted journalists, not to mention cops. Have you any suggestions?'

'Yes. You told me yesterday morning that a man you know named Austin Byne had phoned to ask you to take his place at that gathering. Today Mr Laidlaw said that a man named Austin Byne, Mrs Robilotti's nephew, had once gone to Grantham House on an errand for his aunt. I suppose the same man?'

'You suppose.' I crossed my legs. 'It wouldn't hurt you any, and would be good for my morale, if you let me take a trick now and then. Austin Byne had already occurred to me, and I asked for suggestions only to be polite. I already know what your powers of observation and memory are and you didn't have to demonstrate them by remembering that I had mentioned his name on the fly and – Why the snort?'

'At the notion that your morale needs any encouragement. Do you know where to reach Mr Byne?'

I said I did and, before resuming at the typewriter, dialled his number. No answer. During the next hour and a half I interrupted my typing four times to dial the number, and still no answer. By then it was dinner-time. For himself, Wolfe will permit nothing and no one to interfere with the course of a meal, and, since we dine together in the dining-room, my leaving the table is a sort of interference and he doesn't like it, but that time I had to. Three times during dinner I went to the office to dial Byne's number, with no luck, and I tried again when, having finished the baked pears, we transferred to the office and Fritz brought coffee. I accept a 'no answer' verdict only after counting thirteen rings, and had got nine when the doorbell rang and Fritz announced Saul Panzer. The other two came a minute later.

That trio, the three that Wolfe always called on when we needed more eyes and ears and legs, were as good as you could get in the metropolitan area. In fact, Saul Panzer, a little guy with a big nose who never wore a hat, compromising on a cap when the weather was rough, was better. With an office and a staff he could have cleaned up, but that wouldn't have left him enough time for playing the piano or playing pinochle or keeping up with his reading, so he preferred to freelance at seventy bucks a day. Fred Durkin, bulky and bald-headed, had his weak points, but he was worth at least half as much as Saul, which was his price, if you gave him the right kind of errands. If Orrie Cather had been as smart as he was brave and handsome he would have been hiring people instead of being hired, and Wolfe would have had to find someone else, which wouldn't have been easy because good operatives are scarce.

They were on yellow chairs in a row facing Wolfe's desk. We hadn't seen any of them for two months, and civilities had been exchanged, including handshakes. They are three of the nine or ten people to whom Wolfe willingly offers a hand. Saul and Orrie had accepted offers of coffee; Fred had preferred beer.

Wolfe sipped coffee, put his cup down, and surveyed them. 'I have undertaken,' he said, 'to find an explanation for something that can't possibly be explained.'

Fred Durkin frowned, concentrating. He had decided long ago that there was a clue in every word Wolfe uttered, and he wasn't going to miss one if he could help it. Orrie Cather smiled to show that he recognized a gag when he heard it, and finally appreciated it. Saul Panzer said, 'Then the job is to invent one.'

Wolfe nodded. 'It may come to that, Saul. Either that or aban‑don it. Usually, as you know, I merely give you specific assign‑ments, but in this case you will have to be told the situation and the background. We are dealing with the death of a woman named Faith Usher who drank poisoned champagne at the home of Mrs Robert Robilotti. I suppose you have heard of it.'

They all had.

Wolfe drank coffee. 'But you should know all that I know, ex‑cept the identity of my client. Yesterday morning Archie got a phone call from a man he knows, by name Austin Byne, the nephew of Mrs Robilotti. He asked Archie . . .'

Seeing that I could be spared for a while, and thinking it was time for another try at Byne, I got up, circled around the trio, went to the kitchen, and dialled the number on the extension there. After five rings I was thinking I was going to draw a blank again, but then I had a voice saying hallo.

'Byne?' I asked. 'Dinky Byne?'

'Who is this?'

'Archie Goodwin.'

'Oh, hallo there. I've been thinking you might call. To give me hell for getting you into a mess. I don't blame you. Go on and say it.'

'I could all right, but I've got another idea. You said you'd return the favour some day, and tomorrow is the day. I want to run up to Grantham House and have a talk with someone there, preferably the woman in charge, and they're probably having too many visitors and won't let me in. So I thought you might say a word for me – on the phone, or write a letter I can take, or maybe even go along. How about it?'

Silence. Then: 'What makes you think a word from me would help?'

'You're Mrs Robilotti's nephew. And I heard somebody say, I forget who, that she has sent you there on errands.'

Another silence. 'What are you after? What do you want to talk about?'

'I'm just curious about something. Some questions the cops have asked me because I was there last night, the mess you got me into, have made me curious.'

'What questions?'

'That's a long story. Also complicated. Just say I'm nosy by nature, that's why I'm in the detective business. Maybe I'm trying to scare up a client. Anyway, I'm not asking you to attend a death by poisoning, as you did me, though you didn't know it. I just want you to make a phone call.'

'I can't, Archie.'

'No? Why not?'

'Because I'm not in a position to. It wouldn't be – It might look as if – I mean I just can't do it.'

'Okay, forget it. I'll have to feed some other curiosity – I've got plenty. For instance, my curiosity about why you asked me to fill in for you because you had such a cold you could hardly talk when you didn't have a cold – at least not the kind you tried to fake. I haven't told the cops about that, your faking the cold, so I guess I'd better do that and ask them to ask you why. I'm curious.'

'You're crazy. I did have a cold. I wasn't faking.'

'Nuts. Take care of yourself. I'll be seeing you, or the cops will.'

Silence, a short one. 'Don't hang up, Archie.'

'Why not? Make an offer.'

'I want to talk this over. I want to see you, but I don't want to leave here because I'm expecting a phone call. Maybe you could come here?'

'Where is here?'

'My apartment. Eighty-seven Bowdoin Street, in the Village. It's two blocks south –'

'I know where it is. I'll be there in twenty minutes. Take some aspirin.'

When I had hung up, Fritz, who was at the sink, turned to say, 'As I thought, Archie. I knew there would be a client, since you were there.'

I told him I'd have to think that over to decide how to take it, and went to the office to tell the conference it would have to manage without me for a while.

Chapter 7

There's no telling what 87 Bowdoin Street had been like a few years back – or rather, there is, if you know the neighbourhood – but someone had spent some dough on it, and it wasn't at all bad when you got inside. The tile floor was a nice dark green, the walls were a lighter green but the same tone, and the frame of the entrance for the do-it-yourself elevator was outlined with a plain wide strip of dull aluminium. Having been instructed over the intercom in the vestibule, I entered the elevator and pushed the button marked 5.

When I emerged on the fifth floor Byne was there to greet me and ushered me in. After taking my hat and coat he motioned me through a doorway, and I found myself in a room that I would have been perfectly willing to move to when the day came that Wolfe fired me or I quit, with perhaps a few minor changes. The rugs and chairs were the kind I like, and the lights were okay, and there was no fireplace. I hate fireplaces. When Byne had got me in a chair and asked if I would like a drink, and I had declined with thanks, he stood facing me. He was tall and lanky and loose-jointed, with not much covering for his face bones except skin.

'That was a hell of a mess I got you into,' he said. 'I'm damn sorry.'

'Don't mention it,' I told him. 'I admit I wondered a little why you picked me. If you want some free advice, free but good, next time you want to cook up a reason for skipping something, don't overdo it. If you make it a cold, not that kind of a cold, just a plain everyday virus.'

He turned a chair around and sat. 'Apparently you've convinced yourself that was a fake.'

'Sure I have, but my convincing myself doesn't prove anything. The proof would have to be got, and of course it could be if it mattered enough – items like people you saw or talked to Monday evening, or phoned to yesterday or they phoned you, and whoever keeps this place so nice and clean, if she was here yesterday – things like that. That would be for the cops. If I needed any proof personally, I got it when as soon as I mentioned that the cold was a fake you had to see me right away. So why don't we just file that?'

'You said you haven't told the cops.'

'Right. It was merely a conclusion I had formed.'

'Have you told anyone else? My aunt?'

'No. Certainly not her. I was doing you a favour, wasn't I?'

'Yes, and I appreciate it. You know that, Archie, I appreciate it.'

'Good. We all like to be appreciated. I would appreciate knowing what it is you want to talk over.'

'Well.' He clasped his hands behind his head, showing how casual it was, just a pair of pals chatting free and easy. 'To tell the truth, I'm in a mess too. Or I will be if you'd like to see me squirm. Would you like to see me squirm?'

'I might if you're a good squirmer. How do I go about it?'

'All you have to do is spill it about my faking a cold. No matter who you spill it to it will get to my aunt, and there I am.' He unclasped his hands and leaned forward. 'Here's how it was. I've gone to those damn annual dinners on my uncle's birthday the last three years and I was fed up, and when my aunt asked me again I tried to beg off, but she insisted, and there are reasons why I couldn't refuse. But Monday night I played poker all night, and yesterday morning I was fuzzy and couldn't face it. The question was who to tap. For that affair it can't be just anybody. The first two candidates I picked were out of town, and the next three all had dates. Then I thought of you. I knew you could handle yourself in any situation, and you had met my aunt. So I called you, and you were big-hearted enough to say yes.'

He sat back. 'That's how it was. Then this morning comes the news of what happened. I said I was sorry I got you into it, and I am, I'm damned sorry, but frankly, I'm damned glad I wasn't there. It certainly wasn't a pleasant experience, and I'm just selfish enough to be glad I missed it. You'll understand that.'

'Sure. Congratulations. I didn't enjoy it much myself.'

'I'll bet you didn't. So that's what I wanted, to explain how it was, so you'd see it wouldn't help matters any for anyone to know about my faking a cold. It certainly wouldn't help me, because it would get to my aunt sooner or later, and you know how she'd be about a thing like that. She'd be sore as hell.'

I nodded. 'I don't doubt it. Then it's an ideal situation. You want something from me, and I want something from you. Perfect. We'll swap. I don't broadcast about the phoney cold, and you get me an audience at Grantham House. What's that woman's name? Irving?'

'Irwin. Blanche Irwin.' He scratched the side of his neck with a forefinger. 'You want to swap, huh?'

'I do. What could be fairer?'

'It's fair enough,' he conceded. 'But I told you on the phone I'm not in a position to do that.'

'Yeah, but then I was asking a favour. Now I'm making a deal.'

His neck itched again. 'I might stretch a point. I might, if I knew what you want with her. What's the idea?'

'Greed. Desire for dough. I've been offered five hundred dollars for an eye-witness story on last night, and I want to decorate it with some background. Don't tell Mrs Irwin that, though. She's probably down on journalists by now. Just tell her I'm your friend and a good loyal citizen and have only been in jail five times.'

He laughed. 'That'll do it all right. Wait till you see her.' He sobered. 'So that's it. It's a funny world, Archie. A girl gets herself in a fix she sees only one way out of, to kill herself, and you're there to see her do it just because I had had all I wanted of those affairs, and here you're going to collect five hundred dollars just because you were there. It's a funny world. So I didn't do you such a bad turn after all.'

I had to admit that was one way of looking at it. He said he felt like saluting the funny world with a drink, and wouldn't I join him, and I said I'd be glad to. When he had gone and brought the requirements, a scotch and water for me and bourbon on the rocks for him, and we had performed the salute, he got at the phone and made a person-to-person call to Mrs Irwin at Grantham House. Apparently there was nothing at all wrong with his position; he merely told her he would appreciate it if she would see a friend of his, and that was all there was to it. She said morning would be better than afternoon. After he hung up we discussed the funny world while finishing the drinks, and when I left one more step had been taken towards the brotherhood of man.

Back home, the conference was over, the trio had gone, and Wolfe was at his desk with his current book, one he had said I must read, *World Peace through World Law*, by Grenville Clark and Louis B. Sohn. He finished a paragraph, lowered it, and told me to enter expense advances to Saul and Fred and Orrie, two hundred dollars each. I went to the safe for the book and made the entries, returned the book, locked the safe, and asked him if I needed to know anything about their assignments. He said that could wait, meaning that he wanted to get on with his reading, and asked about mine. I told him it was all set, that he wouldn't see me in the morning because I would be leaving for Grantham House before nine.

'I now call Austin Byne "Dinky," ' I told him. 'I suppose because he's an inch over six feet, but I didn't ask. I should report that he balked and I had to apply a little pressure. When he phoned yesterday he tried to sound as if his tubes were clogged, but he boggled it. He had no cold. He now says that he had been to three of those affairs and had had enough, and he rang me only after he had tried five others and they weren't available. So we made a deal. He gets me in at Grantham House, and I won't tell his aunt on him. He seems to feel that his aunt might bite.'

Wolfe grunted. 'Nothing is as pitiable as a man afraid of a woman. Is he guileless?'

'I would reserve it. He is not a dope. He might be capable of knowing that someone was going to kill Faith Usher so that it would pass for suicide, and he wanted somebody there alert and brainy and observant to spot it, so he got me, and he is now counting on me, with your help, to nail him. Or her. Or he may be on the level and merely pitiable.'

'You and he have not been familiar?'

'No, sir. Just acquaintances. I have only seen him at parties.'

'Then his selecting you is suggestive *per se*.'

'Certainly. That's why I took the trouble to go to see him. To observe. There were other ways of getting to Mrs Irwin of Grantham House.'

'But you have formed no conclusion.'

'No, sir. Question mark.'

'Very well. Pfui. Afraid of a woman.' He lifted his book, and I went to the kitchen for a glass of milk.

At eight-twenty the next morning, Thursday, I was steering the 1957 Heron sedan up the Forty-sixth Street ramp to the West Side Highway. Buying the sedan, the year before, had started an argument that wasn't finished yet. Wolfe pays for the cars, but I do the driving, and I wanted one I could U-turn when the occasion arose, and that clashed with Wolfe's notion that anyone in a moving vehicle was in constant deadly peril, and that the peril was in inverse ratio to the size of the vehicle. In a forty-ton truck he might actually have been able to relax. So we got the Heron, and I must say that I had nothing against it but its size.

I soon had proof of what I had been hearing and reading, that the forty-eight-hour rain in New York had been snow a little to the north. At Hawthorne Circle it was already there at the roadside, and the farther I rolled on the Taconic State Parkway the more there was of it. The sun was on it now, glancing off the slopes of the drifts and banks, and it was very pleasant, fighting the hardships of an old-fashioned winter by sailing along on the concrete at fifty-eight m.p.h. with ridges of white four and five feet high only a step from the hubcaps. When I finally left the parkway and took a secondary road through the hills, the hardships closed in on me some for a few miles, and when I turned in at an entrance between two stone pillars, with 'Grantham House' on one of them, and headed up a curving driveway climbing a hill, only a single narrow lane had been cleared, and as I rounded a sharp curve the hubcaps scraped the ridge.

Coming out of another curve, I braked and stopped. I was blocked, though not by snow. There were nine or ten of them standing there facing me, pink-faced and bright-eyed in the sunshine, in an assortment of jackets and coats, no hats, some with gloves and some without. They would have been taken anywhere for a bunch of high-school girls except for one thing: they were all too bulky around the middle. They stood and grinned at me, white teeth flashing.

I cranked the window down and stuck my head out. 'Good morning. What do you suggest?'

One in front, with so much brown hair that only the middle of her face showed, called out, 'What paper are you from?'

'No paper. I'm sorry if I ought to be. I'm just an errand boy. Can you get by?'

Another one, a blonde, had advanced to the fender. 'The trouble is,' she said, 'that you're right in the centre. If you edge over we can squeeze past.' She turned and commanded, 'Back up and give him room.'

They obeyed. When they were far enough away I eased the car forward and to the right until the fender grazed the snowbank, and stopped. They said that was fine and started down the alley single file. As they passed the front fender they turned sidewise, every darned one, which seemed to me to be faulty tactics, since their spread fore and aft was more than from side to side. Also they should have had their backs to the car so their fronts would be against the soft snow, but no, they all faced me. A couple of them made friendly remarks as they went by, and one with a sharp little chin and dancing dark eyes reached in and pulled my nose. I stuck my head out to see that they were all clear, waved good-bye, and pressed gently on the gas.

Grantham House, which had once been somebody's mansion, sprawled over about an acre, surrounded by evergreen trees loaded with snow and other trees still in their winter skeletons. A space had been cleared with enough room to turn around, barely, and I left the car there, followed a path across a terrace to a door, opened it, entered, crossed the vestibule, and was in a hall about the size of Mrs Robilotti's drawing-room. A man who would never see eighty again came hobbling over, squeaking at me, 'What's your name?'

I told him. He said Mrs Irwin was expecting me, and led me into a smaller room where a woman was sitting at a desk. As I entered she spoke, with a snap. 'I hope to goodness you didn't run over my girls.'

'Absolutely not,' I assured her. 'I stopped to let them by.'

'Thank you.' She motioned to a chair. 'Sit down. The snow has tried to smother us, but they have to get air and exercise. Are you a newspaperman?'

I told her no and was going to elaborate, but she had the floor. 'Mr Byne said your name is Archie Goodwin and you're a friend of his. According to the newspaper there was an Archie Goodwin at that party at Mrs Robilotti's. Was that you?'

I was at a disadvantage. With her smooth hair, partly grey, her compact little figure, and her quick brown eyes wide apart, she reminded me of Miss Clark, my high-school geometry teacher out in Ohio, and Miss Clark had always had my number. I had waited until I saw her to decide just what line to take. First I had to decide whether to say it was me or it was I.

'Yes,' I said, 'that was me. It also said in the paper that I work for a private detective named Nero Wolfe.'

'I know it did. Are you here as a detective?'

She certainly liked to come to the point. So had Miss Clark. But I hoped I was man enough not to be afraid of a woman. 'The best way to answer that,' I told her, 'is to explain why I came. You know what happened at that party and you know I was there. The idea seems to be that Faith Usher committed suicide. I have got the impression that the police may settle for that. But on account of what I saw, and what I didn't see, I doubt it. My personal opinion is that she was murdered, and if she was, I would hate to see whoever did it get away with it. But before I start howling about it in public I want to do a little checking, and I thought the best place to check on Faith Usher herself was here with you.'

'I see.' She sat straight and her eyes were straight. 'Then you're a knight with a plume?'

'Not at all. I'd feel silly with a plume. My pride is hurt. I'm a professional detective and I try to be a good one, and I believe that someone committed murder right before my eyes, and how do you think I like that?'

'Why do you believe it was murder?'

'As I said, on account of what I saw and what I didn't see. A question of observation. I would prefer to let it go at that if you don't mind.'

She nodded. 'The professional with his secrets. I have them too; I have a medical degree. Did Mrs Robilotti send you here?'

That decision wasn't hard to make. Grantham House wasn't dependent on Mrs Robilotti, since it had been provided for by Albert Grantham's will, and it was ten to one that I knew what Mrs Irwin thought of Mrs Robilotti. So I didn't hesitate.

'Good heavens, no. To have a suicide in her drawing-room was bad enough. If she knew I was here looking for support for my belief that it was murder she'd have a fit.'

'Mrs Robilotti doesn't have fits, Mr Goodwin.'

'Well, you know her better than I do. If she ever did have a fit this would call for one. Of course, I may be sticking my neck out. If you prefer suicide to murder as much as she does I've wasted a lot of gas driving up here.'

She looked at me, sizing me up. 'I don't,' she said bluntly.

'Good for you,' I said.

She lifted her chin. 'I see no reason why I shouldn't tell you what I have told the police. Of course, it's possible that Faith did kill herself, but I doubt it. I get to know my girls pretty well, and she was here nearly five months, and I doubt it. I knew about the bottle of poison she had – she didn't tell me, but one of the other girls did – and that was a problem, whether to get it away from her. I decided not to, because it would have been dangerous. As long as she had it and went on showing it and talking about using it, that was her outlet for her nerves, and if I took it away she would have to get some other outlet, and there was no telling what it might be. One reason I doubt if she killed herself is that she still had that bottle of poison.'

I smiled. 'The police would love that.'

'They didn't, naturally. Another reason is that if she had finally decided to use the poison she wouldn't have done it there at that party, with all those people. She would have done it somewhere alone, in the dark, and she would have left a note for me. She knew how I felt about my girls, and she would have known it would hurt me, and she would have left a note. Still another reason is the fact that she was actually pretty tough. That bottle of poison was merely the enemy that she intended to defeat somehow – it was death, and she was going to conquer it. The spirit she had, down deep, showed sometimes in a flash in her eyes. You should have seen that flash.'

'I did, Tuesday evening when I was dancing with her.'

'Then she still had it, and she didn't kill herself. But how are you going to prove it?'

'I can't. I can't prove a negative. I would have to prove an affirmative, or at least open one up. If she didn't poison her champagne someone else did. Who? That's the target.'

'Oh.' Her eyes widened. 'Good heavens! That's obvious, certainly, but if you'll believe me, Mr Goodwin, it hadn't occurred to me. My only thought was that Faith had not killed herself. My mind had stopped there.' Her lips tightened. She shook her head. 'I can't help it,' she said emphatically. 'I wish you success, anyhow. I would help you if I could.'

'You already have,' I assured her, 'and maybe you can more. If you don't mind a few questions. Since you've read the paper, you know who was there Tuesday evening. About the three girls – Helen Yarmis, Ethel Varr, and Rose Tuttle – they were all here at the time Faith Usher was, weren't they?'

'Yes. That is, the times overlapped. Helen and Ethel left a month before Faith did. Rose came six weeks before Faith left.'

'Had any of them known her before?'

'No. I didn't ask them – I ask the girls as few questions as possible about their past – but there was no indication that they had, and there isn't much going on here that I don't know about.'

'Did any trouble develop between any of them and her?'

She smiled. 'Now, Mr Goodwin. I said I would help you if I could, but this is ridiculous. My girls have their squabbles and their peeves, naturally, but I assure you that nothing that happened here put murder into the heart of Helen or Ethel or Rose. If it had I would have known it, and I would have dealt with it.'

'Okay. If it wasn't one of them I'll have to look elsewhere. Take the three male guests – Edwin Laidlaw, Paul Schuster, and Beverly Kent. Do you know any of them?'

'No. I had never heard their names before.'

'You know nothing about them?'

'Nothing whatever.'

'What about Cecil Grantham?'

'I haven't seen him for several years. His father brought him twice – no, three times – to our summer picnic, when Cecil was in his middle teens. After his father died he was on our Board of Directors for a year, but he resigned.'

'You know of no possible connection between him and Faith Usher?'

'No.'

'What about Robert Robilotti?'

'I have seen him only once, more than two years ago, when he came to our Thanksgiving dinner with Mrs Robilotti. He played the piano for the girls and had them singing songs, and when Mrs Robilotti was ready to leave, the girls didn't want him to go. My feelings were mixed.'

'I'll bet they were. Faith Usher wasn't here then?'

'No.'

'Well, we're all out of men. Celia Grantham?'

'I knew Celia fairly well at one time. For a year or so after she finished college she came here frequently, three or four times a month, to teach the girls things and talk with them; then suddenly she quit. She was a real help and the girls liked her. She has fine qualities, or had, but she is headstrong. I haven't seen her for four years. I am tempted to add something.'

'Go ahead.'

'I wouldn't if I thought you would misunderstand. You are looking for a murderer, and Celia would be quite capable of murder if she thought the occasion demanded it. The only discipline she recognizes is her own. But I can't imagine an occasion that would have led her to kill Faith Usher. I haven't seen her for four years.'

'Then if she had had contact with Faith Usher you wouldn't know about it. Least but not last, Mrs Robilotti.'

'Well.' She smiled. 'She is Mrs Robilotti.'

I smiled back. 'I agree. You certainly have known her. She was Mrs Albert Grantham. I am tempted to add something.'

'You may.'

'I wouldn't if I thought you would misunderstand. I feel that if you knew anything that would indicate that Mrs Robilotti might have killed Faith Usher you would think it was your duty to tell me about it. So I can simply ask, do you?'

'That's rather cheeky, Mr Goodwin. But I simply answer, I do

76

not. Ever since Mr Grantham died Mrs Robilotti has been coming here about once a month except when she was travelling, but she has never been at ease with the girls, nor they with her. Of course she came while Faith was here, but as far as I know she never spoke with her except as one of a group. So my answer to your question is no.'

'Who picks the girls to be invited to the annual dinner on Grantham's birthday?'

'When Mr Grantham was alive, I did. The first few years after he died, Mrs Grantham did, on information I supplied. The last two years she has left it to Mr Byne, and he consults me.'

'Is that so? Dinky didn't mention that.'

' "Dinky"?'

'Mr Byne. We call him that. I'll ask him about it. But if you don't mind telling me, how does he do it? Does he suggest names and ask you about them?'

'No, I make a list, chiefly of girls who have been here in the past year, with information and comments, and he chooses from that. I make the list with care. Some of my girls would not be comfortable in those surroundings. On what basis Mr Byne makes his selections, I don't know.'

'I'll ask him.' I put a hand on her desk. 'And now for the main point, what I was mostly counting on if you felt like helping me. It's very likely that the event or the situation, whatever it was, that led to Faith Usher's death dated from before she came here. It could have happened after she left, but you wouldn't know about that anyway. She was here nearly five months. You said you ask the girls as few questions as possible about their pasts, but they must tell you a lot, don't they?'

'Some of them do.'

'Of course. And of course you keep it in confidence. But Faith is dead, and you said you'd help me if you could. She must have told you things. She may even have told you the name of the man who was responsible for her being here. Did she?'

I asked that because I had to. Mrs Irwin was much too smart not to realize that that was the first and foremost question a detective would want answered about Faith Usher's past, and if I hadn't asked it she would have wondered why and might even have been bright enough to suspect that I already knew. There wasn't much chance that she had the answer, in view of her tone and manner when she said that she had never heard of Edwin Laidlaw.

'No,' she said. 'She never said a word about him to me, and I doubt if she did to any of the girls.'

'But she did tell you things?'

'Not very much. If you mean facts, people she had known and things she had done, really nothing. But she talked with me a good deal, and I formed two conclusions about her – I mean about her history. No, three. One was that she had had only one sexual relationship with a man, and a brief one. Another was that she had never known her father and probably didn't know who he was. The third was that her mother was still alive and that she hated her – no, hate is too strong a word. Faith was not a girl for hating. Perhaps the word is repugnance. I made those three conclusions, but she never stated any of them explicitly. Beyond that I know nothing about her past.'

'Do you know her mother's name?'

'No. As I said, I have no facts.'

'How did she get to Grantham House?'

'She came here one day in March, just a year ago. She was in her seventh month. No letter or phone call, she just came. She said she had once read about Grantham House in a magazine and she remembered it. Her baby was born on May eighteenth.' She smiled. 'I don't have on my tongue the dates of all the births here, but I looked it up for the police.'

'Is there any possibility that the baby is involved? I mean in her death? Anything or anyone connected with it or its adoption?'

'Not the slightest. Absolutely none. I handle that. You may take my word for it.'

'Did she ever have any visitors here?'

'No. Not one.'

'You say she was here five months, so she left in August. Did someone come for her?'

'No. Usually the girls don't stay so long after the baby comes, but Faith had rather a bad time and had to get her strength back. Actually someone did come for her – Mrs James Robbins, one of our directors, drove her to New York. Mrs Robbins had got a job for her at Barwick's, the furniture store, and had arranged for her to share a room with another girl, Helen Yarmis. As you know, Helen was there Tuesday evening. Helen might know if anything – Yes, Dora?'

I turned my head. The woman who had opened the door – middle-aged and a little too plump for her blue uniform – stood holding the knob. She spoke. 'I'm sorry to interrupt, Doctor, but Katherine may be going to rush things a bit. Four times since nine o'clock, and the last one was only twenty minutes.'

Mrs Irwin was out of her chair and moving. By the time she reached me I was up too, to take the hand she offered.

'It may be only a prelude,' she said, 'but I'd better go and see. I repeat, Mr Goodwin, I wish you success, in spite of what success would mean. I don't envy you your job, but I wish you success. You'll forgive me for rushing off.'

I told her I would, and I could have added that I'd rather have my job than hers, or Katherine's either. As I got my coat from a chair and put it on I figured that if she had been there fifteen years and had averaged one a week Katherine's would be the 780th, or even at two a month it would be the 360th ... On my way out to the car I had a worry. If I met the girls on their way back the manoeuvre would have to be repeated with me headed downhill and them up, and I didn't like the idea of them rubbing their fronts along the side of the car again, with the door handles. But luckily, as I started the engine, here they came, straggling from the tunnel of the driveway into the cleared space. Their faces were even pinker and they were puffing. One of them sang out, 'Oh, are you going?' and another one called, 'Why don't you stay for lunch?' I told them some other time. I was glad I had turned the car around on arrival. I had an impulse to tell them Katherine was tuning up for her big act to see how they would take it, but decided it wouldn't be tactful, and when they had cleared the way I fed gas and rolled. The only one who didn't tell me good-bye was out of breath.

Chapter 8

When we have company in the office I like to be there when they arrive, even if the matter being discussed isn't very important or lucrative, but that time I missed it by five minutes. When I got there at five past six that afternoon Wolfe was behind his desk, Orrie Cather was in my chair, and Helen Yarmis, Ethel Varr, and Rose Tuttle were there in three of the yellow chairs facing Wolfe. As I entered, Orrie got up and moved to the couch. He has not entirely given up the idea that some day my desk and chair will be his for good, and he liked to practise sitting there when I am not present.

Not that it had taken me six hours to drive back from Grantham House. I had got back in time to eat my share of lunch, kept warm by Fritz, and then had given Wolfe a verbatim report of my talk with Mrs Irwin. He was sceptical of my opinion that her mind was sound and her heart was pure, since he is convinced that every woman alive has a screw loose somewhere, but he had to agree that she had talked to the point, she had furnished a few hints that might be useful about some of our cast of characters, and she had fed the possibility that Austin Byne might not be guileless. Further discourse with Dinky was plainly indicated. I dialled his number and got no answer, and, since he might be giving his phone a recess, I took a walk through the sunshine, first to the bank to deposit Laidlaw's cheque and then down to 87 Bowdoin Street.

Pushing Byne's button in the vestibule got no response. I had suggested to Wolfe that I might take along an assortment of keys so that if Byne wasn't home I could go on in and pass the time by looking around, but Wolfe had vetoed it, saying that Byne had not yet aroused our interest quite to that point. So I spent a long hour and a quarter in a doorway across the street. That's one of the most tiresome chores in the business, waiting for someone to show when you have no idea how long it will be and you haven't much more idea whether he has anything that will help.

It was twelve minutes past five when a taxi rolled to a stop at the curb in front of 87 and Byne climbed out. When he turned after paying the hackie, I was there.

'We must share a beam,' I told him. 'I feel a desire to see you, and come, and here you are.'

Something had happened to the brotherhood of man. His eye was cold. 'What the hell – ' he began, and stopped. 'Not here,' he said. 'Come on up.'

Even his manners were affected. He entered the elevator ahead of me, and upstairs, though he let me precede him into the apartment, I had to deal with my coat and hat unaided. Inside, in the room that would require only minor changes, my fanny was barely touching the chair seat when he demanded, 'What's this crap about murder?'

'That word "crap" bothers me,' I said. 'The way we used it when I was a boy out in Ohio, we knew exactly what it meant. But I looked it up in the dictionary once, and there's no – '

'Nuts.' He sat. 'My aunt says that you're saying that Faith Usher was murdered, and that on account of you the police won't accept the fact that it was suicide. You know damn well it was suicide. What are you trying to pull?'

'No pull.' I clasped my hands behind my head, showing it was just a pair of pals chatting free and easy, or ought to be. 'Look, Dinky. You are neither a cop nor a district attorney. I have given them a statement of what I saw and heard at that party Tuesday evening, and if you want to know why that makes them go slow on their verdict you'll have to ask them. If I told them any lies they'll catch up with me and I'll be hooked. I'm not going to start an argument with you about it.'

'What did you say in your statement?'

I shook my head. 'Get the cops to tell you. I won't. I'll tell you this: if my statement is all that keeps them from calling it suicide, I'm the goat. I'll be responsible for a lot of trouble for that whole bunch, and I don't like it but can't help it. So I'm doing a little checking on my own. That's why I wanted to see Mrs Irwin at Grantham House. I told you I had been offered five hundred bucks for a story on Faith Usher, and I had, but what I was really after was information on whether anyone at that party might have had any reason to kill her. For example, if someone intended to kill her at that party he had to know she would be there. So I wanted to ask Mrs Irwin how she had been picked to be invited and who had picked her.'

I gave him a friendly grin. 'And I asked her and she told me, and that was certainly no help, since it was you, and you weren't at the party. You even faked a cold to get out of going – and by the way, I said I wouldn't broadcast that, and I haven't.' I thought it wouldn't hurt to remind him that there was still a basis for brotherhood.

'I know,' he said, 'you've got that to shake at me. About my picking Faith Usher to be invited, I suppose Mrs Irwin told you how it was done. I know she told the police. She gave me a list of names with comments, and I merely picked four of the names. I've just been down at the District Attorney's office telling them about it. As I explained to them, I had no personal knowledge of any of those girls. From Mrs Irwin's comments I just picked the ones that seemed to be the most desirable.'

'Did you keep the list? Have you got it?'

'I had it, but an assistant district attorney took it. One named Mandelbaum. No doubt he'll show it to you if you ask him.'

I ignored the dig. 'Anyway,' I said, 'even if the comments showed that you stretched a point to pick Faith Usher, that wouldn't cross any Ts, since you skipped the party. Did anyone happen to be with you when you were making the selections? Someone who said something like, "there's one with a nice name, Faith Usher, a nice unusual name, why don't you ask her?" '

'No one was with me. I was alone.' He pointed. 'At that desk.'

'Then that's out.' I was disappointed. 'If you don't mind my asking, a little point occurred to me as I was driving back from Grantham House – that you were interested enough to take the trouble to pick the girls to be invited, but not enough to go to the party. You even went to a lot of trouble to stay away. That seemed a little inconsistent, but I suppose you can explain it.'

'To you? Why should I?'

'Well, explain it to yourself and I'll listen.'

'There's nothing to explain. I picked the girls because my aunt asked me to. I did it last year too. I told you last night why I skipped the party.' He cocked his head, making the skin even tighter on his cheekbone. 'What the hell are you driving at, anyhow? Do you know what I think?'

'No, but I'd like to. Tell me.'

He hesitated. 'I don't mean that, exactly, what I think. I mean what my aunt thinks – or I'll put it this way, an idea she's got in her mind. I guess she hasn't forgotten that remark you made once that she resented. Also she feels that Wolfe overcharged her for that job he did. The idea is that if you have sold the police and the District Attorney on your murder theory, and if they make things unpleasant enough for her and her guests you and Wolfe might figure that she would be willing to make a big contribution to have it stopped. A contribution that would make you remember something that would change their minds. What do you think of that?'

'It *is* an idea,' I conceded, 'but it has a flaw. If I remembered something now that I didn't put in my statement, no contribution from your aunt would replace my hide that the cops and the D.A. would peel off. Tell your aunt that I appreciate the compliment and her generous offer, but I can't –'

'I didn't say she made an offer. You keep harping on your damn statement. What's in it?'

That was what was biting him, naturally, as it had bit Celia Grantham and Edwin Laidlaw, and probably all of them. For ten minutes he did the harping on it. He didn't go so far as to make a cash offer, either on his own or on behalf of his aunt, but he appealed to everything from my herd instinct to my better nature. I would have let him go on as long as his breath lasted, on the chance that he might drop a word with a spark of light in it, if I hadn't known that company was expected at the office at six o'clock and I wanted to be there when they arrived. When I left he was so frustrated he didn't even go to the hall with me.

I had shaved it pretty close, and that was the worst time of day for uptown traffic, so I didn't quite make it. It was six-five when I climbed out of the taxi and headed for the stoop. If you think I was straining my nerves more than necessary, you don't know Wolfe as I do. I have seen him get up and march out and take to his elevator merely because a woman has burst into tears or started screaming at him, and the expected company, he had told me, was three females, Helen Yarmis, Ethel Varr, and Rose Tuttle, and there was no telling what shape they might be in after the sessions they had been having with various officers of the law.

Therefore I was relieved when I entered the office and found that everything was peaceful, with Wolfe at his desk, the girls in a row facing him, and Orrie in my chair. As I greeted the guests Orrie moved to the couch, and when I was where I belonged Wolfe addressed me.

'We have only exchanged civilities, Archie. Have you anything that should be reported?'

'Nothing that won't wait, no, sir. He is still afraid of a woman.'

He went to the company. 'As I was saying, ladies, I thank you for coming. You were under no obligation. Mr Cather, asking you to come, explained that Mr Goodwin's opinion, expressed in your hearing Tuesday evening, that Faith Usher was murdered, has produced some complications that are of concern to me, and that I wished to consult with you. Mr Goodwin still believes –'

'I told him,' Rose Tuttle blurted, 'that Faith might take the poison right there, and he said he would see that nothing happened, but it did.' Her blue eyes and round face weren't as cheerful as they had been at the party, in fact they weren't cheerful at all, but her curves were all in place and her pony tail made its jaunty arc.

Wolfe nodded. 'He has told me of that. But he thinks that what happened was not what you feared. He still believes that someone else poisoned Miss Usher's champagne. Do you disagree with him, Miss Tuttle?'

'I don't know. I thought she might do it, but I didn't see her. I've answered so many questions about it that now I don't know what I think.'

'Miss Varr?'

You may remember my remark that I would have picked Ethel Varr if I had been shopping. Since she was facing Wolfe and I had her in profile, and she was in daylight from the windows, her face wasn't ringing any of the changes in its repertory, but that was a good angle for it, and the way she carried her head would never change. Her lips parted and closed again before she answered.

'I don't think,' she said in a voice that wanted to tremble but she wouldn't let it, 'that Faith killed herself.'

'You don't, Miss Varr? Why?'

'Because I was looking at her. When she took the champagne and drank it. I was standing talking with Mr Goodwin, only just then we weren't saying anything because Rose had told me that she had told him about Faith having the poison, and he was watching Faith so I was watching her too, and I'm sure she didn't put anything in the champagne because I would have seen her. The police have been trying to get me to say that Mr Goodwin told me to say that, but I keep telling them that he couldn't because he hasn't said anything to me at all. He hasn't had a chance to.' Her head turned, changing her face, of course, as I had it straight on. 'Have you, Mr Goodwin?'

I wanted to go and give her a hug and a kiss, and then go and shoot Cramer and a few assistant district attorneys. Cramer hadn't seen fit to mention that my statement had had corroboration; in fact, he had said that if it wasn't for me suicide would be a reasonable assumption. The damn liar. After I shot him I would sue him for damages.

'Of course not,' I told her. 'If I may make a personal remark, you told me at the dinner table that you were only nineteen years old and hadn't learned how to take things, but you have certainly learned how to observe things, and how to take your ground and stand on it.' I turned to Wolfe. 'It wouldn't hurt any to tell her it's satisfactory.'

'It is,' he acknowledged. 'Indeed, Miss Varr, quite satisfactory.' That, if she had only known it, was a triumph. He gave me a satisfactory only when I hatched a masterpiece. His eyes moved. 'Miss Yarmis?'

Helen Yarmis still had her dignity, but the corners of her wide, curved mouth were apparently down for good, and since that was her best feature she looked pretty hopeless. 'All I can do,' she said stiffly, 'is say what I think. I think Faith killed herself. I told her it was dumb to take that poison along to a party where we were supposed to have a good time, but I saw it there in her bag. Why would she take it along to a party like that if she wasn't going to use it?'

Wolfe's understanding of women has some big gaps, but at least he knows enough not to try using logic on them. He merely ignored her appeal to unreason. 'When,' he asked, 'did you tell her not to take the poison along?'

'When we were dressing to go to the party. We lived in an apartment together. Just a big bedroom with a kitchenette, and the bathroom down the hall, but I guess that's an apartment.'

'How long had you and she been living together?'

'Seven months. Since August, when she left Grantham House. I can tell you anything you want to ask, after the way I've been over it the last two days. Mrs Robbins brought her from Grantham House on a Friday so she could get settled to go to work at Barwick's on Monday. She didn't have many clothes –'

'If you please, Miss Yarmis. We must respect the convenience of Miss Varr and Miss Tuttle. During those seven months did Miss Usher have many callers?'

'She never had any.'

'Neither men nor women?'

'No. Except once a month when Mrs Robbins came to see how we were getting along, that was all.'

'How did she spend her evenings?'

'She went to school four nights a week to learn typing and shorthand. She was going to be a secretary. I never saw how she could if she was as tired as I was. Fridays we often went to the movies. Sundays she would go for walks, that's what she said. I was too tired. Anyway, sometimes I had a date, and –'

'If you please. Did Miss Usher have no friends at all? Men or women?'

'I never saw any. She never had a date. I often told her that was no way to live, just crawl along like a worm –'

'Did she get any mail?'

'I don't know, but I don't think so. The mail was downstairs on a table in the hall. I never saw her write any letters.'

'Did she get any telephone calls?'

'The phone was downstairs in the hall, but of course I would have known if she got a call when I was there. I don't remember she ever got one. This is kinda funny, Mr Wolfe. I can answer your questions without even thinking because they're all the same questions the police have been asking, even the same words, so I don't have to stop to think.'

I could have given her a hug and kiss too, though not in the same spirit as with Ethel Varr. Anyone who takes Wolfe down a peg renders a service to the balance of nature, and to tell him to his face that he was merely a carbon copy of the cops was enough to spoil his appetite for dinner.

He grunted. 'Every investigator follows a routine up to a point, Miss Yarmis. Beyond that point comes the opportunity for talent if any is at hand. I find it a little difficult to accept your portfolio of negatives.' Another grunt. 'It may not be outside my capacity to contrive a question that will not parrot the police. I'll try. Do you mean to tell me that during the seven months you lived with Miss Usher you had no inkling of her having any social or personal contact – excluding her job and night school and the visits of Mrs Robbins – with any of her fellow beings?'

Helen was frowning. The frown deepened. 'Say it again,' she commanded.

He did so, slower.

'They didn't ask that,' she declared. 'What's an inkling?'

'An intimation. A hint.'

She still frowned. She shook her head. 'I don't remember any hints.'

'Did she never tell you that she had met a man that day that she used to know? Or a woman? Or that someone, perhaps a customer at Barwick's, had annoyed her? Or that she had been accosted on the street? Did she never account for a headache or a fit of ill humour by telling of an encounter she had had? An encounter is a meeting face to face. Did she never mention a single name in connection with some experience, either pleasant or disagreeable? In all your hours together, did nothing ever remind her – What is it?'

Helen's frown had gone suddenly, and the corners of her mouth had lifted a little. 'Headache,' she said. 'Faith never had head-aches, except only once, one day when she came home from work. She wouldn't eat anything and she didn't go to school that night, and I wanted her to take some aspirin but she said it wouldn't help any. Then she asked me if I had a mother, and I said my mother was dead and she said she wished hers was. That didn't sound like her and I said that was an awful thing to say, and she said she knew it was but I might say it too if I had a mother like hers, and she said she had met her on the street when she was out for lunch and there had been a scene, and she had to run to get away from her.' Helen was looking pleased. 'So that was a contact, wasn't it?'

'It was. What else did she say about it?'

'That was all. The next day – no, the day after – she said she was sorry she had said it and she hadn't really meant it, about wishing her mother was dead. I told her if all the people died that I had wished they were dead there wouldn't be room in the cemeteries. Of course that was exaggerated, but I thought it would do her good to know that people were wishing people were dead all the time.'

'Did she ever mention her mother again?'

'No, just that once.'

'Well. We have recalled one contact, perhaps we can recall another.'

But they couldn't. He contrived other questions that didn't parrot the police, but all he got was a collection of blanks, and finally he gave it up.

He moved his eyes to include the others. 'Perhaps I should have explained,' he said, 'exactly why I wanted to talk with you. First, since you had been in close association with Miss Usher, I wanted to know your attitude towards Mr Goodwin's opinion that she did not kill herself. On the whole you have supported it. Miss Varr has upheld it on valid grounds, Miss Yarmis has opposed it on ambiguous grounds, and Miss Tuttle is uncertain.'

That was foxy and unfair. He knew damn well Helen Yarmis wouldn't know what 'ambiguous' meant, and that was why he used it.

He was going on. 'Second, since I am assuming that Mr Goodwin is right, that Miss Usher did not poison her champagne and that therefore someone else did, I wanted to look at you and hear you talk. You are three of the eleven people who were there and are suspect; I exclude Mr Goodwin. One of you might have taken that opportunity to use a lump of the poison that you all knew – '

'But we couldn't!' Rose Tuttle blurted. 'Ethel was with Archie

Goodwin. Helen was with that publisher, what's-his-name, Laid-law, and I was with the one with big ears – Kent. So we couldn't!'

Wolfe nodded. 'I know, Miss Tuttle. Evidentially, nobody could, so I must approach from another direction, and all eleven of you are suspect. I don't intend to harass you ladies in an effort to trick you into betraying some guarded secret of your relationship with Miss Usher; that's an interminable and laborious process and all night would only start it; and besides, it would probably be futile. If one of you has such a secret it will have to be exposed by other means. But I did want to look at you and hear you talk.'

'I haven't talked much,' Ethel Varr said.

'No,' Wolfe agreed, 'but you supported Mr Goodwin, and that alone is suggestive. Third – and this was the main point – I wanted your help. I am assuming that if Miss Usher was murdered you would wish the culprit to be disclosed. I am also assuming that none of you has so deep an interest in any of the other eight people there that you would want to shield him from exposure if he is guilty.'

'I certainly haven't,' Ethel Varr declared. 'Like I told you, I'm sure Faith didn't put anything in her champagne, and if she didn't, who did? I've been thinking about it. I know it wasn't me, and it wasn't Mr Goodwin, and I'm sure it wasn't Helen or Rose. How many does that leave?'

'Eight. The three male guests, Laidlaw, Schuster, and Kent. The butler. Mr Grantham and Miss Grantham. Mr and Mrs Robilotti.'

'Well, I certainly don't want to shield any of *them*.'

'Neither do I,' Rose Tuttle asserted, 'if one of them did it.'

'You couldn't shield them,' Helen Yarmis told them, 'if they *didn't* do it. There wouldn't be anything to shield them from.'

'You don't understand, Helen,' Rose told her. 'He wants to find out who it was. Now, for instance, what if it was Cecil Grantham, and what if you saw him take the bottle out of Faith's bag and put it back, or something like that, would you want to shield him? That's what he wants to know.'

'But that's just it,' Helen objected. 'If Faith did it herself, why would I want to shield him?'

'But Faith didn't do it. Ethel and Mr Goodwin were both look-ing at her.'

'Then why,' Helen demanded, 'did she take the bottle to the party when I told her not to?'

Rose shook her head, wiggling the pony tail. 'You'd better explain it,' she told Wolfe.

'I fear,' he said, 'that it's beyond my powers. It may clear the air a little if I say that a suspicious word or action at the party, like Mr Grantham's taking the bottle from the bag, was not what I had in mind. I meant, rather, to ask if you know anything about any of those eight people that might suggest the possibility of a reason why one of them might have wanted Miss Usher to die. Do you know of any connection between one of them and Miss Usher – either her or someone associated with her?'

'I don't,' Rose said positively.

'Neither do I,' Ethel declared.

'There's so many of them,' Helen complained. 'Who are they again?'

Wolfe, patient under stress, pronounced the eight names.

Helen was frowning again. 'The only connection I know about,' she said, 'is Mrs Robilotti. When she came to Grantham House to see us. Faith didn't like her.'

Rose snorted. 'Who did?'

Wolfe asked. 'Was there something definite, Miss Yarmis? Something between Miss Usher and Mrs Robilotti?'

'I guess not,' Helen conceded. 'I guess it wasn't any more definite with Faith than it was with the rest of us.'

'Did you have in mind something in particular that Miss Usher and Mrs Robilotti said to each other?'

'Oh, no. I never heard Faith say anything to her at all. Neither did I. She thought we were harlots.'

'Did she use that word? Did she call you harlots?'

'Of course not. She tried to be nice but didn't know how. One of the girls said that one day when she had been there, she said that she thought we were harlots.'

'Well.' Wolfe took in air, in and clear down to his middle, and let it out again. 'I thank you again, ladies, for coming.' He pushed his chair back and rose. 'We seem to have made little progress, but at least I have seen and talked with you, and I know where to reach you if the occasion arises.'

'One thing I don't see,' Rose Tuttle said as she left her chair. 'Mr Goodwin said he wasn't there as a detective, but he *is* a detective, and I had told him about Faith having the poison, and I should think he ought to know exactly what happened. I didn't think anyone could commit a murder with a detective right there.'

A very superficial and half-baked way to look at it, I thought, as I got up to escort the ladies out.

Chapter 9

Paul Schuster, the promising young corporation lawyer with the thin nose and quick dark eyes, sat in the red leather chair at a quarter past eleven Friday morning, with the eyes focused on Wolfe. 'We do not claim,' he said, 'to have evidence that you have done anything that is actionable. It should be clearly understood that we are not presenting a threat. But it is a fact that we are being injured, and if you are responsible for the injury it may become a question of law.'

Wolfe moved his head to take the others in – Cecil Grantham, Beverly Kent, and Edwin Laidlaw, lined up on yellow chairs – and to include them. 'I am not aware,' he said dryly, 'of having inflicted an injury on anyone.'

Of course that wasn't true. What he meant was that he hadn't inflicted the injury he was trying to inflict. Forty-eight hours had passed since Laidlaw had written his cheque for twenty thousand dollars and put it on Wolfe's desk, and we hadn't earned a dime of it, and the prospect of ever earning it didn't look a bit brighter. Dinky Byne's cover, if he had anything to cover, was intact. The three unmarried mothers had supplied no crack to start a wedge. Orrie Cather, having delivered them at the office for consultation, had been given another assignment, and had come Thursday evening after dinner, with Saul Panzer and Fred Durkin, to report; and all it had added up to was an assortment of blanks. If anyone had had any kind of connection with Faith Usher, it had been buried good and deep, and the trio had been told to keep digging.

When, a little after ten Friday morning, Paul Schuster had phoned to say that he and Grantham and Laidlaw and Kent wanted to see Wolfe, and the sooner the better, I had broken two of the standing rules: that I make no appointments without checking with Wolfe, and that I disturb him in the plant rooms only for emergencies. I had told Schuster to be there at eleven, and I had buzzed the plant rooms on the house phone to tell Wolfe that company was coming. When he growled I told him that I had looked up 'emergency' in the dictionary, and it meant an unforeseen combination of circumstances which calls for immediate action, and if he wanted to argue either with the dictionary or with me I was willing to go upstairs and have it out. He had hung up on me.

And was now telling Schuster that he was not aware of having inflicted an injury on anyone.

'Oh, for God's sake,' Cecil Grantham said.

'Facts are facts,' Beverly Kent muttered. Unquestionably a diplomatic way of putting it, suitable for a diplomat. When he got a little higher up the ladder he might refine it by making it 'A fact is a fact is a fact.'

'Do you deny,' Schuster demanded, 'that we owe it to Goodwin that we are being embarrassed and harassed by a homicide investigation? And he is your agent, employed by you. No doubt you know the legal axiom, *respondeat superior*. Isn't that an injury?'

'Not only that,' Cecil charged, 'but he goes up to Grantham House, sticking his nose in. And yesterday a man tried to pump my mother's butler, and he had no credentials, and I want to know if you sent him. And another man with no credentials is asking questions about me among my friends, and I want to know if you sent *him*.'

'To me,' Beverly Kent stated, 'the most serious aspect is the scope of the police inquiry. My work on our Mission to the United Nations is in a sensitive field, very sensitive, and already I have been definitely injured. Merely to have been present when a sensational event occurred, the suicide of that young woman, would have been unfortunate. To be involved in an extended police inquiry, a murder investigation, could be disastrous for me. If in addition to that you are sending your private agents among my friends and associates to inquire about me, that is adding insult to injury. I have no information of that, as yet. But you have, Cece?'

Cecil nodded. 'I sure have.'

'So have I,' Schuster said.

'Have you, Ed?'

Laidlaw cleared his throat. 'No direct information, no. Nothing explicit. But I have reason to suspect it.'

He handled it pretty well, I thought. Naturally he had to be with them, since if he had refused to join in the attack they would have wondered why, but he wanted Wolfe to understand that he was still his client.

'You haven't answered my question,' Schuster told Wolfe. 'Do you deny that we owe this harassment to Goodwin, and therefore to you, since he is your agent?'

'No,' Wolfe said. 'But you owe it to me, through Mr Goodwin, only secondarily. Primarily you owe it to the man or woman who murdered Faith Usher. So it's quite possible that one of you owes it to himself.'

'I knew it,' Cecil declared. 'I told you, Paul.'

Schuster ignored him. 'As I said,' he told Wolfe, 'this may become a question of law.'

'I expect it to, Mr Schuster. A murder trial is commonly regarded as a matter of law.' Wolfe leaned forward, flattened his palms on the desk, and sharpened his tone. 'Gentlemen. Let's get to the point, if there is one. What are you here for? Not, I suppose, merely to grumble at me. To buy me off? To bully me? To dispute my ground? What are you after?'

'Goddammit,' Cecil demanded, 'what are *you* after? That's the point! What are you trying to pull? Why did you send –'

'Shut up, Cece,' Beverly Kent ordered him, not diplomatic at all. 'Let Paul tell him.'

The lawyer did so. 'Your insinuation,' Schuster said, 'that we have entered into a conspiracy to buy you off is totally unwarranted. Or to bully you. We came because we feel, with reason, that our rights of privacy are being violated without provocation or just cause, and that you are responsible. We doubt if you can justify that responsibility, but we thought you should have a chance to do so before we consider what steps may be taken legally in the matter.'

'Pfui,' Wolfe said.

'An expression of contempt is hardly an adequate justification, Mr Wolfe.'

'I didn't intend it to be, sir.' Wolfe leaned back and clasped his fingers at the apex of his central mound. 'This is futile, gentlemen, both for you and for me. Neither of us can possibly be gratified. You want a stop put to your involvement in a murder inquiry, and my concern is to involve you as deeply as possible – the innocent along with –'

'Why?' Schuster demanded. 'Why are you concerned?'

'Because Mr Goodwin's professional reputation and competence have been challenged, and by extension my own. You invoked *respondeat superior*; I will not only answer, I will act. That the innocent must be involved along with the guilty is regrettable but unavoidable. So you can't get what you want, but no more can I. What I want is a path to a fact. I want to know if one of you has buried in his past a fact that will account for his resort to murder to get rid of Faith Usher, and if so, which. Manifestly you are not going to sit here and submit to a day-long inquisition by me, and even if you did, the likelihood that one of you would betray the existence of such a fact is minute. So, as I say, this is futile both for you and for me. I wish you good day only as a matter of form.'

But it wasn't quite that simple. They had come for a show-down, and they weren't going to be bowed out with a 'good day' as a matter of form – at least, three of them weren't. They got pretty well worked up before they left. Schuster forgot all about saying that they hadn't come to present a threat. Kent went far beyond the bounds of what I would call diplomacy. Cecil Grantham blew his top, at one point even pounding the top of Wolfe's desk with his fist. I was on my feet, to be handy in case one of them lost control and picked up a chair to throw but my attention was mainly on our client. He was out of luck. For the sake of appearance he sort of tried to join in, but his heart wasn't in it, and all he could manage was a mumble now and then. He didn't leave his chair until Cecil headed for the door, followed by Kent, and then, not wanting to be the last one out, he jumped up and went. I stepped to the hall to see that no one took my new hat in the excitement, went and tried the door after they were out, and returned to the office.

I expected to see Wolfe leaning back with his eyes closed, but no. He was sitting up straight, glaring at space. He transferred the glare to me.

'This is grotesque,' he growled.

'It certainly is,' I agreed warmly. 'Four of the suspects come to see you uninvited, all set for a good long heart-to-heart talk, and what do they get? Bounced. The trouble is, one of them was our client, and he may think we're loafing on the job.'

'Bah. When the men phone tell them to come in at three. No. At two-thirty. No. At two o'clock. We'll have lunch early. I'll tell Fritz.' He got up and marched out.

I felt uplifted. That he was calling the men in for new instructions was promising. That he had changed it from three o'clock, when his lunch would have been settled, to two-thirty, when digestion would have barely started, was impressive. That he had advanced it again, to two, with an early lunch, was inspiring. And then to go to tell Fritz instead of ringing for him – all hell was popping.

Chapter 10

'How many times,' Wolfe asked, 'have you heard me confess that I am a witling?'

Fred Durkin grinned. A joke was a joke. Orrie Cather smiled. He was even handsomer when he smiled, but not necessarily braver. Saul Panzer said, 'Three times when you meant it, and twice when you didn't.'

'You never disappoint me, Saul.' Wolfe was doing his best to be sociable. He had just crossed the hall from the dining-room. With Fred and Orrie he wouldn't have strained himself, but Saul had his high regard. 'This, then,' he said, 'makes four times that I have meant it and this time my fault was so egregious that I made myself pay for it. The only civilized way to spend the hour after lunch is with a book, but I have just swallowed my last bite of cheese cake, and here I am working. You must bear with me. I am paying a deserved penalty.'

'Maybe it's our fault too,' Saul suggested. 'We had an order and we didn't fill it.'

'No,' Wolfe said emphatically. 'I can't grab for the straw of your charity. I am an ass. If any share of the fault is yours it lies in this, that when I explained the situation to you Wednesday evening and gave you your assignments none of you reminded me of my maxim that nothing is to be expected of tagging the footsteps of the police. That's what you've been doing, at my direction, and it was folly. There are scores of them, and only three of you. You have been merely looking under stones that they have already turned. I am an ass.'

'Maybe there's no other stones to try,' Orrie observed.

'Of course there are. There always are.' Wolfe took time to breathe. More oxygen was always needed after a meal unless he relaxed with a book. 'I have an excuse, naturally, that one approach was closed to my ingenuity. By Mr Cramer's account, and Archie didn't challenge it, no one could possibly have poisoned that glass of champagne with any assurance that it would get to Miss Usher. I could have tackled that problem only by a minute examination of everyone who was there, and most of them were not available to me. Sooner or later it must be solved, but only after disclosure of a motive. That was the only feasible approach open to me, to find the motive, and you know what I did. I sent you men to flounder around on ground that the police had already covered, or were covering. Pfui.'

'I saw four people,' Fred protested, 'that the cops hadn't got to.'

'And learned?'

'Well – nothing.'

Wolfe nodded. 'So. The quarry, as I told you Wednesday evening, was evidence of some significant association of one of those people with Miss Usher. That was a legitimate line of inquiry, but it was precisely the one the police were following, and I offer my apologies. We shall now try another line, where you will at least be on fresh ground. I want to see Faith Usher's mother. You are to find her and bring her.'

Fred and Orrie pulled out their notebooks. Saul had one but rarely used it. The one inside his skull was usually all he needed.

'You won't need notes,' Wolfe said. 'There is nothing to note except the bare fact that Miss Usher's mother is alive and must be somewhere. This may lead nowhere, but it is not a resort to desperation. Whatever circumstance in Miss Usher's life resulted in her death, she must have been emotionally involved, and I have been apprised of only two phenomena which importantly engaged her emotions. One was her experience with the man who begot her infant. A talk with him might be fruitful, but if he can be found the police will find him; of course they're trying to. The other was her relationship with her mother. Mrs Irwin, of Grantham House, told Archie that she had formed the conclusion, from talking with Miss Usher, that her mother was alive and that she hated her. And yesterday Miss Helen Yarmis, with whom Miss Usher shared an apartment the last seven months of her life, told me that Miss Usher had come home from work one day with a headache and had said that she had encountered her mother on the street and there had been a scene, and she had had to run to get away from her; and that she wished her mother was dead. Miss Yarmis's choice of words.'

Fred, writing in his notebook, looked up. 'Does she spell Irwin with an E or an I?'

Wolfe always tried to be patient with Fred, but there was a limit. 'As you prefer,' he said. 'Why spell it at all? I've told you all she said that is relevant, and all that I know. I will add that I doubt if either Mrs Irwin or Miss Yarmis mentioned Miss Usher's mother to the police, so in looking for her you shouldn't be jostled.'

'Is her name Usher?' Orrie asked. Of course Saul wouldn't have asked it, and neither would Fred.

'You should learn to listen, Orrie,' Wolfe told him. 'I said that's all I know. And no more is to be expected from either Mrs Irwin or Miss Yarmis. They know no more.' His eyes went to Saul. 'You will direct the search, using Fred and Orrie as occasions arise.'

'Do we keep covered?' Saul asked.

'Preferably, yes. But don't preserve your cover at the cost of missing your mark.'

'I took a look,' I said, 'at the Manhattan phone book when I got back from Grantham House yesterday. A dozen Ushers are listed. Of course she doesn't have to be named Usher, and she doesn't have to live in Manhattan, and she doesn't have to have a phone. It wouldn't take Fred and Orrie long to check the dozen. I can call Lon Cohen at the *Gazette*. He might have gone after the mother for an exclusive and a picture.'

'Sure,' Saul agreed. 'If it weren't for cover my first stop would be the morgue. Even if her daughter hated her, the mother may have claimed the body. But they know me there, and Fred and Orrie too, and of course they know Archie.'

It was decided, by Wolfe naturally, that that risk should be taken only after other tries had failed, and that calling Lon Cohen should obviously come first, and I dialled and got him. It was a little complicated. He had rung me a couple of times to try to talk me into the eye-witness story, and now my calling to ask if he had dug up Faith Usher's mother aroused all his professional instincts. Was Wolfe working on the case, and if so, on behalf of whom? Had someone made me a better offer for a story, and did I want the mother so I could put her in, and who had offered me how much? I had to spread the salve thick, and assure him that I wouldn't dream of letting anyone but the *Gazette* get my by-line, and promise that if and when we had anything fit for publication he would get it, before he would answer my simple question.

I hung up and swivelled to report. 'You can skip the morgue. A woman went there Wednesday afternoon to claim the body. Name, Marjorie Betz. B-E-T-Z. Address, Eight-twelve West Eighty-seventh Street, Manhattan. She had a letter signed by Elaine Usher, mother of Faith Usher, same address. By her instructions the body was delivered this morning to the Metropolitan Crematory on Thirty-ninth Street. A *Gazette* man has seen Marjorie Betz, but she clammed up and is staying clammed. She says Elaine Usher went somewhere Wednesday night and she doesn't know where she is. The *Gazette* hasn't been able to find her, and Lon thinks nobody else has. End of chapter.'

'Fine,' Saul said. 'Nobody skips for nothing.'

'Find her,' Wolfe ordered. 'Bring her. Use any inducement that seems likely to – '

The phone rang, and I swivelled and got it.

'Nero Wolfe's office, Arch – '

'Goodwin?'

'Yes.'

'This is Laidlaw. I've got to see Wolfe. Quick.'

'He's here. Come ahead.'

'I'm afraid to. I just left the District Attorney's office and got a taxi, and I'm being followed. I was on my way to see Wolfe about what happened at the District Attorney's office but now I can't because they mustn't know I'm running to Wolfe. What do I do?'

'Any one of a dozen things. Shaking a tail is a cinch, but of course you haven't had any practice. Where are you?'

'In a booth in a drugstore on Seventh Avenue near Sixteenth Street.'

'Have you dismissed your taxi?'

'Yes. I thought that was better.'

'It was. How many men are in the taxi tailing you?'

'Two.'

'Then they mean it. Okay, so do we. First, have a Coke or

something to give me time to get a car – say, six or seven minutes. Then take a taxi to Two-fourteen East Twenty-eighth Street. The Perlman Paper Company is there on the ground floor.' I spelled Perlman. 'Got that?'

'Yes.'

'Go in and ask for Abe and say to him, "Archie wants some more candy." What are you going to say to him?'

'Archie wants some more candy.'

'Right. He'll take you on through to Twenty-seventh Street, and when you emerge I'll be there in front, either at the curb or double-parked, in a grey Heron sedan. Don't hand Abe anything, he wouldn't like it. This is part of our personalized service.'

'What if Abe isn't there?'

'He will be, but if he isn't don't mention candy to anyone else. Find a booth and ring Mr Wolfe.'

I hung up, scribbled 'Laidlaw' on my pad, tore the sheet off, and got up and handed it to Wolfe. 'He wants to see you quick,' I said, 'and needs transportation. I'll be back with him in half an hour or less.'

He nodded, crumpled the sheet, and dropped it in his waste-basket; and I wished the trio luck on their mother hunt and went.

At the garage, at the corner of Tenth Avenue, I used the three minutes while Hank was bringing the car down to go to the phone in the office and ring the Perlman Paper Company, and got Abe. He said he had been wondering when I would want more candy and would be glad to fill the order.

The de-tailing operation went fine, without a hitch. Going cross-town on Thirty-fourth Street, it was a temptation to swing down Park or Lexington to Twenty-eighth, so as to pass Number 214 and see if I recognized the two in the taxi, but since they might also recognize me I vetoed it and gave them plenty of room by continuing to Second Avenue before turning downtown, then west on Twenty-seventh. It was at the rear entrance on Twenty-seventh that the Perlman Paper Company did its loading and unloading, but no truck was there when I arrived, and I rolled to the curb at 2.49, just nineteen minutes since Laidlaw had phoned, and at 2.52 here he came trotting across the sidewalk. I opened the door and he piled in.

He looked upset. 'Relax,' I told him as I fed gas. 'A tail is a trifle. They won't go in to ask about you for at least half an hour, if at all, and Abe will say he took you to the rear to show you some stock, and you left that way.'

'It's not the tail. I want to see Wolfe.' His tone indicated that his plan was to get him down and tramp on him, so I left him to his mood. Crossing town, I considered whether there was enough of a chance that the brownstone was under surveillance to warrant taking him in the back way, through the passage between buildings on Thirty-fourth Street, decided no, and went up Eighth Avenue to Thirty-fifth. As usual, there was no space open in front of the brownstone, so I went on to the garage and left the car, and walked back with him. When we entered the office I was at his heels. He didn't have the build to get Wolfe's bulk down and trample on it without help, but after all, he was the only one of the bunch, as it stood then, who had had dealings with Faith Usher that might have produced a motive for murder, and if a man has once murdered you never know what he'll do next.

He didn't move a finger. In fact, he didn't even move his tongue. He stood at the corner of Wolfe's desk looking down at him, and after five seconds I realized that he was too mad, or too scared, or both, to speak, and I took his elbow and eased him to the red leather chair and into it.

'Well, sir?' Wolfe asked.

The client pushed his hair back, though he must have known by then that it was a waste of energy. 'I may be wrong,' he croaked. 'I hope to God I am. Did you send a note to the District Attorney telling him that I am the father of Faith Usher's child?'

'No.' Wolfe's lips tightened. 'I did not.'

Laidlaw's head jerked to me. 'Did you?'

'No. Of course not.'

'Have you told anybody? Either of you?'

'Plainly,' Wolfe said, 'you are distressed and so must be indulged. But nothing has happened to release either Mr Goodwin or me from our pledge of confidence. If and when it does you will first be notified. I suggest that you retire and cool off a little.'

'Cool off, hell.' The client rubbed the chair arms with his palms, eyeing Wolfe. 'Then it wasn't you. All right. When I left here this morning I went to my office, and my secretary said the District Attorney's office had been trying to reach me, and I phoned and was told they wanted to see me immediately, and I went. I was taken in to Bowen, the District Attorney himself, and he asked if I wished to change my statement that I had never met Faith Usher before Tuesday evening, and I said no. Then he showed me a note that he said had come in the mail. It was typewritten. There wasn't any signature. It said, "Have you found out yet that Edwin Laidlaw is the father of Faith Usher's baby? Ask him about his trip to Canada in August nineteen fifty-six." Bowen didn't let me take it. He held on to it. I sat and stared at it.'

Wolfe grunted. 'It was worth a stare, even if it had been false. Did you collapse?'

'No! By God, I didn't! I don't think I decided what to do while I sat there staring at it; I think my subconscious mind had already decided what to do. Sitting there staring at it, I was too stunned to decide anything, so I must have already decided that the only thing to do was refuse to answer any questions about anything at all, and that's what I did. I said just one thing: that whoever sent that note had libelled me and I had a right to find out who it was, and to do that I would have to have the note, but of course they wouldn't give it to me. They wouldn't even give me a copy. They kept at me for two hours, and when I left I was followed.'

'You admitted nothing?'

'No.'

'Not even that you had taken a trip to Canada in August of nineteen fifty-six?'

'No. I admitted *nothing*. I didn't answer a single question.'

'Satisfactory,' Wolfe said. 'Highly satisfactory. This is indeed welcome, Mr Laidlaw. We have –'

'Welcome!' the client squawked. '*Welcome?*'

'Certainly. We have at last goaded someone to action. I am gratified. If there was any small shadow of doubt that Miss Usher was murdered, this removes it. They have all claimed to have had no knowledge of Miss Usher prior to that party; one of them lied, and he has been driven to move. True, it is still possible that you yourself are the culprit, but I now think it extremely improbable. I prefer to take it that the murderer has felt compelled to create a diversion, and that is most gratifying. Now he is doomed.'

'But good God! They know about – about me!'

'They know no more than they knew before. They get a dozen accusatory unsigned letters every day, and have learned that the charges in most of them are groundless. As for your refusal to answer questions, a man of your standing might be expected to take that position until he got legal advice. It's a neat situation, very neat. They will of course make every effort to find confirmation of that note, but it is a reasonable assumption that no one can supply it except the person who sent the note, and if he dares to do so we'll have him. We'll challenge him, but we'll have him.' He glanced up at the wall clock. 'However, we shall not merely twiddle our thumbs and wait for that. I have thirty minutes. You told me Wednesday morning that no one on earth knew of your dalliance with Miss Usher; now we know you were wrong. We must review every moment you spent in her company when you might have been seen or heard. When I leave, at four o'clock, Mr Goodwin will continue with you. Start with the day she first attracted your notice, when she waited on you at Cordoni's. Was anyone you knew present?'

When Wolfe undertakes that sort of thing, getting someone to recall every detail of a past experience, he is worse than a housewife bent on finding a speck of dust that the maid overlooked. Once I sat for eight straight hours, from nine in the evening until daylight came, while he took a chauffeur over every second of a drive, made six months before, to New Haven and back. This time he wasn't quite that fussy, but he did no skipping. When four o'clock came, time for him to go up and play with the orchids, he had covered the episode at Cordoni's, two dinners, one at the Woodbine in Westchester and one at Henke's on Long Island, and a lunch at Gaydo's on Sixty-ninth Street.

I carried on for more than an hour, following Wolfe's *modus operandi* more or less, but my pulse wasn't pounding from the thrill of it. It seemed to me that it could have been handled just as well by putting one question: 'Did you at any time, anywhere, when she was with you, including Canada, see or hear anyone who knew you?' and then make sure there were no gaps in his memory. As for chances that they had been seen but he hadn't known it, there had been plenty. Aside from restaurants, he had had her in his car, in midtown, in daylight, seven times. The morning they left for Canada he had parked his car, with her in it, in front of his club, while he went in to leave a message for somebody.

But I carried on, and we were working on the third day in Canada, somewhere in Quebec, when the doorbell rang and I went to the hall for a look through the one-way glass and saw Inspector Cramer of Homicide.

I wasn't much surprised, since I knew there had been a pointer for them if they were interested enough; and just as Laidlaw's subconscious had made his decision in advance, mine had made mine. I went to the rack and got Laidlaw's hat and coat, stepped back into the office, and told the client, 'Inspector Cramer is here looking for you. This way out. Come on, move –'

'But how did –'

'No matter how.' The doorbell rang. 'Damn it, move!'

He came, and followed me to the kitchen. Fritz was at the big table, doing something to a duck. I told him, 'Mr Laidlaw wants to leave the back way in a hurry, and I haven't time because Cramer wants in. Show him quick, and you haven't seen him.'

Fritz headed for the back door, which opens on our private enclosed garden if you want to call it that, whose fence has a gate into the passage between buildings which leads to Thirty-fourth Street. As the door closed behind them and I turned, the doorbell rang. I went to the front, not in a hurry, put the chain bolt on, opened the door to the two-inch crack the chain allowed, and spoke through it politely.

'I suppose you want me? Since you know Mr Wolfe won't be available until six o'clock.'

'Open up, Goodwin.'

'Under conditions. You know damn well what my orders are: no callers admitted between four and six unless it's just for me.'

'I know. Open up.'

I took that for a commitment, and he knew I did. Also it was conceivable that some character – Sergeant Stebbins, for instance – was on his way with a search warrant, and if so it would take the edge off to admit Cramer without one. So I said, 'Okay, if it's me you want,' removed the bolt, and swung the door wide; and he stepped in, marched down the hall, and entered the office.

I shut the door and went to join him, but by the time I arrived he wasn't there. The connecting door to the front room was open, and in a moment he came through and barked at me, 'Where's Laidlaw?'

I was hurt. 'I thought you wanted me. If I had –'

'Where's Laidlaw?'

'Search me. There's lots of Laidlaws, but I haven't got one. If you mean –'

He made for the door to the hall, passing within arm's length of me en route.

The rules for dealing with officers of the law are contradictory. Whether you may restrain them by force or not depends. It was okay to restrain Cramer from entering the house by the force of the chain bolt. It would have been okay to restrain him from going upstairs if there had been a locked door there and I had refused to open it, but I couldn't restrain him by standing on the first step and not letting him by, no matter how careful I was not to hurt him. That may make sense to lawyers, but not to me.

But that's the rule, and it didn't matter that he had said he knew *our* rules before I let him in. So when he crossed the hall to the stairs I didn't waste my breath to yell at him; I saved it for climbing the three flights, which I did, right behind him. Since he was proving that in a pinch he had no honour and no manners, it would have been no surprise if he had turned left at the first landing to invade Wolfe's room, or right at the second landing to invade mine, but he kept going to the top, and on in to the vestibule.

I don't know whether he is off orchids because Wolfe is on them, or is just colour blind, but on the few occasions that I have seen him in the plant rooms he has never shown the slightest sign that he realizes that the benches are occupied. Of course in that house his mind is always occupied or he wouldn't be there, and that could account for it. That day, in the cool room, long panicles of Odonto-glossums, yellow, rose, white with spots, crowded the aisle on both sides; in the tropical room, Miltonia hybrids and Phalaenopsis splashed pinks and greens and browns clear to the glass above; and in the intermediate room the Cattleyas were grandstanding all over the place as always. Cramer might have been edging his way between rows of dried-up cornstalks.

The door from the intermediate room to the potting room was closed as usual. When Cramer opened it and I followed him in, I didn't stop to shut it but circled around him and raised my voice to announce, 'He said he came to see me. When I let him in he dashed past me to the office and then to the front room and started yapping, "Where's Laidlaw?" and when I told him I had no Laidlaw he dashed past me again for the stairs. Apparently he has such a craving for someone named Laidlaw that his morals are shot.'

Theodore Horstmann, at the sink washing pots, had twisted around for a look, but before I finished was twisted back again, washing pots. Wolfe, at the potting bench inspecting seedlings, had turned full around to glare. He had started the glare at me, but by the time I ended had transferred it to Cramer. 'Are you demented?' he inquired icily.

Cramer stood in the middle of the room, returning the glare. 'Some day,' he said, and stopped.

'Some day what? You will recover your senses?'

Cramer advanced two paces. 'So you're horning in again,' he said. 'Goodwin turns a suicide into a murder, and here you are. Yesterday you had those girls here. This morning you had those men here. This afternoon Laidlaw is called downtown to show him something which he refuses to discuss, and when he leaves he heads for you. So I know he has been here. So I come –'

'If you weren't an inspector,' I cut in, 'I'd say that's a lie. Since you are, make it a fib. You do not know he has been here.'

'I know he hopped a taxi and gave the driver this address, and when he saw he was being followed he went to a booth and phoned, and took another taxi to a place that runs through the block, and left by the other street. Where would I suppose he went?'

'Correction. You *suppose* he has been here.'

'All right, I do.' He took another step, towards Wolfe. 'Have you seen Edwin Laidlaw in the last three hours?'

'This is quite beyond belief,' Wolfe declared. 'You know how rigidly I maintain my personal schedule. You know that I resent any attempt to interfere with these two hours of relaxation. But you get into my house by duplicity and then come charging up here to ask me a question to which you have no right to an answer. So you don't get one. Indeed, in these circumstances, I doubt if you could put a question about anything whatever that I *would* answer.' He turned, giving us the broad expanse of his rear, and picked up a seedling.

'I guess,' I told Cramer sympathetically, 'your best bet would be to get a search warrant and send a gang to look for evidence, like cigarette ashes from the kind he smokes. I know where it hurts. You've never forgotten the day you did come with a warrant and a crew to look for a woman named Clara Fox and searched the whole house, including here, and didn't find her, and later you learned she had been in this room in a packing case, covered with osmundine that Wolfe was spraying water on. So you thought if you rushed up before I could give the alarm you'd find Laidlaw here, and now that he isn't you're stuck. You can't very well demand to know why Laidlaw rushed here to discuss something with Wolfe that he wouldn't discuss downtown. You ought to take your coat off when you're in the house or you'll catch cold when you leave. I'm just talking to be sociable while you collect yourself. Of course Laidlaw was here this morning with the others, but apparently you know that. Whoever told you should –'

He turned and was going. I followed.

Chapter 11

At five minutes past six Saul Panzer phoned. That was routine; when one or more of them are out on a chore they call at noon, and again shortly after six, to report progress or lack of it and to learn if there are new instructions. He said he was talking from a booth in a bar and grill on Broadway near Eighty-sixth Street. Wolfe, who had just come down from the plant rooms, did him the honour of reaching for the phone on his desk to listen in.

'So far,' Saul reported, 'we're only scouting. Marjorie Betz lives with Mrs Elaine Usher at the address on Eighty-seventh Street. Mrs Usher is the tenant. I got in to see Miss Betz by one of the standard lines, and got nowhere. Mrs Usher left Wednesday night, and she doesn't know where she is or when she'll be back. We have seen two elevator men, the janitor, five neighbours, fourteen people in local shops and stores, and a hackie Mrs Usher patronizes, and Orrie is now after the maid, who left at five-thirty. Do you want Mrs Usher's description?'

Wolfe said no and I said yes simultaneously. 'Very well,' Wolfe said, 'oblige him.'

'Around forty. We got as low as thirty-three and as high as forty-five. Five feet six, hundred and twenty pounds, blue eyes set close, oval face, takes good care of good skin, hair was light brown two years ago, now blonde, wears it loose, medium cut. Dresses well but a little flashy. Gets up around noon. Hates to tip. I think that's fairly accurate, but this is a guess with nothing specific, that she has no job but is never short of money, and she likes men. She has lived in that apartment for eight years. Nobody ever saw a husband. Six of them knew the daughter, Faith, and liked her, but it has been four years since they last saw her and Mrs Usher never mentions her.'

Wolfe grunted. 'Surely that will do.'

'Yes, sir. Do we proceed?'

'Yes.'

'Okay. I'll wait to see if Orrie gets anywhere with the maid, and if not I have a couple of ideas. Miss Betz may go out this evening, and the lock on the apartment door is only a Wyatt.'

'The hackie she patronizes,' I said. 'She didn't patronize him Wednesday night?'

'According to him, no. Fred found him. I haven't seen him. Fred thinks he got it straight.'

'You know,' I said, 'you say *only* a Wyatt, but you need more than a paper clip for a Wyatt. I could run up there with an assortment, and we could go into conference – '

'No,' Wolfe said firmly. 'You're needed here.'

For what, he didn't say. After we hung up all he did was ask how I had disposed of Laidlaw and then ask for a report of the hour and a quarter I had spent with him, and I could have covered that in one sentence just by saying it had been a washout. But he kept pecking at it until dinner time. I knew what the idea was, and he knew I knew. It was simply that if I had gone to help Saul with an illegal entry into Elaine Usher's apartment there was a chance, say one in a million, that I wouldn't be there to answer the phone in the morning.

But back in the office after dinner he decided it was about time he exerted himself a little, possibly because he saw my expression when he picked up his book as soon as Fritz had come for the coffee service.

He lowered the book. 'Confound it,' he said, 'I wait to see Mrs Usher not merely because her daughter said she hated her. There is also the fact that she has disappeared.'

'Yes, sir. I didn't say anything.'

'You looked something. I suppose you are reflecting that we have had two faint intimations of the possible identity of the person who sent that communication to the District Attorney.'

'I wasn't reflecting. That's your part. What are the two intimations?'

'You know quite well. One, that Austin Byne told Laidlaw that he had seen Faith Usher at Grantham House. He didn't name her, and Laidlaw did not regard his tone or manner as suggestive, but it deserves notice. Of course, you couldn't broach it with Byne, since that would have betrayed our client's confidence. You still can't.'

I nodded. 'So we file it. What's the other one?'

'Miss Grantham. She gave Laidlaw a bizarre reason for refusing to marry him, that he didn't dance well enough. It is true that women constantly give fantastic reasons without knowing that they are fantastic, but Miss Grantham must have known that that one was. If her real reason was merely that she didn't care enough for him, surely she would have made a better choice for her avowed one, unless she despises him. Does she despise him?'

'No.'

'Then why insult him? It is an insult to decline a proposal of marriage, a man's supreme capitulation, with flippancy. She did that six months ago, in September. It is not idle to conjecture that her real reason was that she knew of his experience with Faith Usher. Is she capable of moral revulsion?'

'Probably, if it struck her fancy.'

'I think you should see her. Apparently you do dance well enough. You should be able, without disclosing our engagement with Mr Laidlaw –'

The phone rang, and I turned to get it, hoping it was Saul to say he needed some keys, but no. Saul is not a soprano. However, it was someone who wanted to see me, with no mention of keys. She just wanted me, she said, right away, and I told her to expect me in twenty minutes.

I hung up and swivelled. 'The timing,' I told Wolfe, 'couldn't have been better. Satisfactory. I suppose you arranged it with her while I was out getting Laidlaw. That was Celia Grantham. She wants to see me. Urgently. Presumably to tell me why she insulted Laidlaw when he asked her to marry him, though she didn't say.' I arose. 'Marvellous timing.'

'Where?' Wolfe growled.

'At her home.' I was on my way, and turned to correct it. 'I mean her mother's home. You have the number.' I went.

Since there were at least twenty possible reasons, excluding personal ones, why Celia wanted to see me, and she had given no hint which it was, and since I would soon know anyhow, it would have been pointless to try to guess, so on the way uptown in a taxi that's what I did. When I pushed the button in the vestibule of the Fifth Avenue mansion I had considered only half of them.

I was wondering which I would be for Hackett, the hired detective or the guest, but he didn't have to face the problem. Celia was there with him and took my coat as I shed it and handed it to him, and then fastened on my elbow and steered me to the door of a room on the right that they called the hall room, and on through it. She shut the door and turned to me.

'Mother wants to see you,' she said.

'Oh?' I raised a brow. 'You said you did.'

'I do, but it only occurred to me after Mother got me to decoy for her. The Police Commissioner is here, and they wanted to see you but thought you might not come, so she asked me to phone you, and I realized I wanted to see you too. They're up in the music room, but first I want to ask you something. What is it about Edwin Laidlaw and that girl? Faith Usher.'

That was turning the tables. Wolfe's idea had been that I might manage, without showing any cards, to find out if she was on to our client's secret, and here she was popping it at me and I had to play ignorant.

'Laidlaw?' I shook my head. 'Search me. Why?'

'You don't know about it?'

'No. Am I supposed to?'

'I thought you would, naturally, since it's you that's making all the trouble. You see, I may marry him some day. If he gets into a bad jam I'll marry him now, since you've turned out to be a skunk. That's based on inside information but is not guaranteed. Are you a skunk?'

'I'll think it over and let you know. What about Laidlaw and Faith Usher?'

'That's what I want to know. They're asking questions of all of us, whether we have any knowledge that Edwin ever knew her. Of course he didn't. I think they got an anonymous letter. The reason I think that, they wanted to type something on our typewriters, all four of them – no, five. Hackett has one, and Cece, and I have, and there are two in Mother's office. Are you thwarting me again? Don't you really know?'

'I do now, since you've told me.' I patted her shoulder. 'Any time you're hard up and need a job, ring me. You have the makings of a lady detective, figuring out why they wanted samples from the typewriters. Did they get them?'

'Yes. You can imagine how Mother liked it, but she let them.'

I patted her shoulder again. 'Don't let it wreck your marriage plans. Undoubtedly they got an anonymous letter, but they're a dime a dozen. Whatever the letter said about Laidlaw, even if it said he was the father of her baby, that proves nothing. People who send anonymous letters are never –'

'That's not it,' she said. 'If he was the father of her baby, that would show that if I married him we could have a family, and I want one. What I'm worried about is his getting in a jam, and you're no help.'

Mrs Irwin had certainly sized her up. She had her own way of looking at things. She was going on. 'So now suit yourself. If you'd rather duck Mother and the Police Commissioner, you know where your hat and coat are. I don't like being used for a decoy, and I'll tell them you got mad and went.'

It was a toss-up. The idea of chatting with Mrs Robilotti had attractions, since she might be stirred up enough by now to say something interesting, but with Police Commissioner Skinner present it would probably be just some more ring-around-a-rosy. However, it might be helpful to know why they had gone to the trouble of using Celia for bait, so I told her I would hate to disappoint her mother, and she escorted me out to the reception hall and on upstairs to the music room, where we had joined the ladies Tuesday evening after going without brandy.

The whole family was there – Cecil standing over by a window, and Mr and Mrs Robilotti and Commissioner Skinner grouped on chairs at the far end, provided with drinks, not champagne. As Celia and I approached, Robilotti and Skinner arose, but not to offer hands. Mrs Robilotti lifted her bony chin, but not getting the effect she had in mind. You can't look down your nose at someone when he is standing and you are sitting.

'Mr Goodwin came up on his own,' Celia said. 'I warned him you were laying for him, but here he is. Mr Skinner, Mr Goodwin.'

'We've met,' the Commissioner said. His tone indicated that it was not one of his treasured memories. He had acquired more grey hairs above his ears and a couple of new wrinkles since I had last seen him, a year or so back.

'I wish to say,' Mrs Robilotti told me, 'that I would have preferred never to permit you in my house again.'

Skinner shook his head at her. 'Now, Louise.' He sat down and aimed his eyes at me. 'This is unofficial, Goodwin, and off the record. Albert Grantham was my close and valued friend. He would have hated to have a thing like this happen in his house, and I owe it to him – '

'Also,' Celia cut in, 'he would have hated to ask someone to come and see him and then not invite him to sit down.'

'I agree,' Robilotti said. 'Be seated, Goodwin.' I didn't know he had the spunk.

'It may not be worth the trouble.' I looked down at Mrs Robilotti. From that slant her angles were even sharper. 'Your daughter said you wanted to see me. Just to tell me I'm not welcome?'

She couldn't look down her nose, but she could look. 'I have just spent,' she said, 'the worst three days of my life, and you are responsible. I had had a previous experience with you, you and the man you work for, and I should have known better than to have you here. I think you are quite capable of blackmail, and I think that's what you have in mind. I want to tell you that I won't submit to it, and if you try – '

'Hold it, Mom,' Cecil called over. 'That's libellous.'

'Also,' Skinner said, 'it's useless. As I said, Goodwin, this is unofficial and off the record. None of my colleagues know I'm here, including the District Attorney. Let's assume something, just an assumption. Let's assume that here Tuesday evening, when something happened that you had said you would prevent, you were exasperated – naturally you would be – and in the heat of the moment you blurted out that you thought Faith Usher had been murdered, and then you found that you had committed yourself. It carried along from the precinct men to the squad men, to Inspector Cramer, to the District Attorney, and by that time you *were* committed.'

He smiled. I knew that smile, and so did a lot of other people. 'Another assumption, merely an assumption. Somewhere along the line, probably fairly early, it occurred to you and Wolfe that some of the people who were involved were persons of wealth and high standing, and that the annoyance of a murder investigation might cause one of them to seek the services of a private detective. If that were a fact, instead of an assumption, it should be apparent to you and Wolfe by now that your expectation is vain. None of the people involved is going to be foolish enough to hire you. There will be no fee.'

'Do I comment as you go along,' I inquired, 'or wait till you're through?'

'Please let me finish. I realize your position. I realize that it would be very difficult for you to go now to Inspector Cramer or the District Attorney and say that upon further consideration you have concluded that you were mistaken. So I have a suggestion. I suggest that you wanted to check, to make absolutely sure of your ground, and came here this evening to inspect the scene again, and found me here. And after a careful inspection – the distances, the positions, and so on – you found that, though you had nothing to apologize for, you had probably been unduly positive. You concede that it is possible that Faith Usher did poison her champagne, and that if the official conclusion is suicide you will not challenge it. I will of course be under an obligation to ensure that you will suffer no damage or inconvenience, that you will not be pestered. I will fulfil that obligation. I know you will probably have to consult with Wolfe before you can give me a definite answer, but I would like to have it as soon as possible. You can phone him from here, or go out to a booth if you prefer, or even go to him. I'll wait here for you. This has gone on long enough. I think my suggestion is reasonable and fair.'

'Are you through?' I asked.

'Yes.'

'Well. I could make some assumptions too, but what's the use? Besides, I'm at a disadvantage. My mother used to tell me never to stay where I wasn't wanted, and you heard Mrs Robilotti. I guess I'm too sensitive, but I've stood it as long as I can.'

I turned and went. Voices came – Skinner's and Celia's and Robilotti's – but I marched on.

Chapter 12

If, to pass the time, you tried to decide what was the most conceited statement you ever heard anybody make, or read or heard of anybody making, what would you pick? The other evening a friend of mine brought it up, and she settled for Louis XIV saying *L'état, c'est moi.* I didn't have to go so far back. Mine, I told her, was 'They know me.' Of course, she wanted to know who said it and when, and since the murderer of Faith Usher had been convicted by a jury just the day before and the matter was closed, I told her.

Wolfe said it that Friday night when I got home and reported. When I finished I made a comment. 'You know,' I said, 'it's pretty damn silly. A police commissioner and a district attorney and an inspector of Homicide all biting nails just because if they say suicide one obscure citizen may let out a squeak.'

'They know me,' Wolfe said.

Beat that if you can. I admit it was justified by the record. They did know him. What if they officially called it suicide, and then, in a day or a week or a month, Wolfe phoned WA9-8241 to tell them to come and get the murderer and the evidence? Not that they were sure that would happen, but past experience had shown them that it was at least an even-money bet that it *might* happen. My point is not that it wasn't justified, but that it would have been more becoming just to describe the situation.

He saved his breath. He said, 'They know me,' and picked up his book.

The next day, Saturday, we had words. The explosion came right after lunch. Saul had phoned at eight-thirty, as I was on my second cup of breakfast coffee, to report no progress. Marjorie Betz had stayed put in the apartment all evening, so the Wyatt lock had not been tackled. At noon he phoned again; more items of assorted information, but still no progress. But at two-thirty, as we returned to the office after lunch, the phone rang and he had news. They had found her. A man from a messenger service had gone to the apartment, and when he came out he had a suitcase with a tag on it. Of course that was pie. Saul and Orrie had entered a subway car right behind him. The tag read: 'Miss Edith Upson, Room 911, Hotel Christie, 523 Lexington Avenue.' The initials 'E.U.' were stamped on the suitcase.

Getting a look at someone who is holed up in a hotel room can be a little tricky, but that situation was made to order. Saul, not encumbered with luggage, had got to the hotel first and gone to the ninth floor, and had been strolling past the door of Room 911 at the moment it opened to admit the messenger with the suitcase; and if descriptions are any good at all, Edith Upson was Elaine Usher. Of course, Saul had been tempted to tackle her then and there, but also of course, since it was Saul, he had retired to think it over and to phone. He wanted to know, were there instructions or was he to roll his own?

'You need a staff,' I told him. 'I'll be there in twelve minutes. Where –'

'No,' Wolfe said, at his phone. 'Proceed, Saul, as you think best. You have Orrie. For this sort of juncture your talents are as good as mine. Get her here.'

'Yes, sir.'

'Preferably in a mood of compliance, but get her here.'

'Yes, sir.'

That was when we had words. I cradled the receiver, not gently, and stood up. 'This is Saturday,' I said, 'and I've got my cheque for this week. I want a month's severance pay.'

'Pfui.'

'No phooey. I am severing relations. It has been eighty-eight hours since I saw that girl die, and your one bright idea, granting that it was bright, was to collect her mother, and I refuse to camp here on my fanny while Saul collects her. Saul is not ten times as smart as I am; he's only twice as smart. A month's severance pay will be –'

'Shut up.'

'Gladly.' I went to the safe for the chequebook and took it to my desk.

'Archie.'

'I have shut up.' I opened the chequebook.

'This is natural. That is, it is in us, and we are alive, and whatever is in life is natural. You are headstrong and I am magisterial. Our tolerance of each other is a constantly recurring miracle. I did not have one idea, bright or not; I had two. We have neglected Austin Byne. It has been two days and nights since you saw him. Since he got you to that party, pretending an ailment he didn't have, and since he told Laidlaw he had seen Miss Usher at Grantham House, and since he chose Miss Usher as one of the dinner guests, he deserves better of us. I suggest that you attend to him.'

I turned my head but kept the chequebook open. 'How? Tell him we don't like his explanations and we want new ones?'

'Nonsense. You are not so ingenuous. Survey him. Explore him.'

'I already have. You know what Laidlaw said. He has no visible means of support, but he has an apartment and a car and plays table-stakes poker and does not go naked. The apartment, by the way, hits my eye. If you hang this murder on him, and if our tolerance miracle runs out of gas, I'll probably take it over. Are you working yourself up to saying that you want to see him?'

'No. I have no lever to use on him. I only feel that he has been neglected. If you approach him again you too will be without a lever. Perhaps the best course would be to put him under surveillance.'

'If I postpone writing this cheque is that an instruction?'

'Yes.'

At least I would get out in the air and away from the miracle for a while. I returned the chequebook to the safe, took twenty tens from the expense drawer, told Wolfe he would see me when he saw me, and went to the hall for my coat and hat.

When starting to tail a man it is desirable to know where he is, so I was a little handicapped. For all I knew, Byne might be in Jersey City or Brooklyn, or some other province, in a marathon poker game, or he might be at home in bed with a cold, or walking in the park. I got air by walking the two miles to Bowdoin Street, and at the corner of Bowdoin and Arbor I found a phone booth and dialled Byne's number. No answer. So at least I knew where he wasn't, and again I had to resist temptation. It is always a temptation to monkey with locks, and one of the best ways to test ears is to enter someone's castle uninvited and, while you are looking here and there for something interesting, listen for footsteps on the stairs or the sound of an elevator. If you don't hear them in time your hearing is defective, and you should try some other line of work when you are out and around again.

Having swallowed the temptation, I moved down the block to a place of business I had noticed Thursday afternoon, with an artistic sign bordered with sweet peas, I think, that said AMY'S NOOK. As I entered, my wristwatch said 4.12. Between then and a quarter past six, slightly over two hours, I ate five pieces of pie, two rhubarb and one each of apple, green tomato, and chocolate, and drank four glasses of milk and two cups of coffee, while seated at a table by the front window, from which I could see the entrance to 87, across the street and up a few doors. To keep from arousing curiosity by either my tenure or my diet, I had my notebook and pencil out and made sketches of a cat sleeping on a chair. In the Village that accounts for anything. The pie, incidentally, was more than satisfactory. I would have liked to take a piece home to Fritz. At six-fifteen the light outside was getting dim, and I asked for my check and was putting my notebook in a pocket when a taxi drew up in front of 87 and Dinky Byne piled out and headed for the entrance. When my change came I added a quarter to the tip, saying, 'For the cat,' and vacated.

It was nothing like as comfortable in the doorway across from 87, the one I had patronized Thursday, but you have to be closer at night than in the daytime, no matter how good your eyes are. I could only hope that Dinky wasn't set to spend the evening curled up with a book, or even without one, but that didn't seem likely, since he would have to eat and I doubted if he did his own cooking. A light had shown at the fifth-floor windows, and that gave me something to do, bend my head back every half-minute or so to see if it had gone out. My neck was beginning to feel the strain when it finally did go out, at 7.02. In a couple of minutes the subject stepped out of the vestibule and turned right.

Tailing a man solo in Manhattan, even if he isn't wise, is a joke. If he suddenly decides to flag a taxi – There are a hundred ifs, and they are all on his side. But of course any game is more fun if the odds are against you, and if you win it's good for the ego. Naturally it's easier at night, especially if the subject knows you. On that occasion I claim no credit for keeping on Byne, for none of the ifs developed. It was merely a ten-minute walk. He turned left on Arbor, crossed Seventh Avenue, went three blocks west and one uptown, and entered a door where there was a sign on the window: TOM'S JOINT.

That's the sort of situation where being known to the subject cramps you; I couldn't go in. All I could do was hunt a post, and I found a perfect one: a narrow passage between two buildings almost directly across the street. I could go in a good ten feet from the building line, where no light came at all, and still see the front of Tom's Joint. There was even an iron thing to sit on if my feet needed a rest.

They didn't. I didn't last long enough. I hadn't been there more than five minutes when suddenly company came. I was alone, and then I wasn't. A man had slid in, caught sight of me, and was peering in the darkness. A question that had arisen on various occasions, which of us had better eyesight, was settled when we spoke simultaneously. He said, 'Archie' and I said, 'Saul'.

'What the hell,' I said.

'Are you on her too?' he asked. 'You might have told me.'

'I'm on a man. I'll be damned. Where is yours?'

'Across the street. Tom's Joint. She just came.'

'This is fate,' I said. 'It is also a break in a thousand. Of course, it could be coincidence. Mr Wolfe says that in a world that operates largely at random, coincidences are to be expected, but not this one. Have you spoken with her? Does she know you?'

'No.'

'My man knows me. His name is Austin Byne. He is six-feet one, hundred and seventy pounds, lanky, loose-jointed, early thirties, brown hair and eyes, skin tight on his bones. Go in and take a look. If you want a bet, one will get you ten that they're together.'

'I never bet against fate,' he said, and went. The five minutes that he was gone were five hours. I sat down on the iron thing and got up again three times, or maybe four.

He came, and said. 'They're together in a booth in a rear corner. No one is with them. He's eating oysters.'

'He'll soon be eating crow. What do you want for Christmas?'

'I have always wanted your autograph.'

'You'll get it. I'll tattoo it on you. Now we have a problem. She's yours and he's mine. Now they're together. Who's in command?'

'That's easy, Archie. Mr Wolfe.'

'I suppose so, damn it. We could wrap it up by midnight. Take them to a basement, I know one, and peel their hides off. If he's eating oysters there's plenty of time to phone. You or me?'

'You. I'll stick here.'

'Where's Orrie?'

'Lost. When she came out he was for feet and I was for wheels, and she took a taxi.'

'I saw it pull up. Okay. Sit down and make yourself at home.'

At the bar and grill at the corner the phone booth was occupied and I had to wait, and I was tired of waiting, having done too much of it in the last four days. But in a few minutes the customer emerged, and I entered, pulled the door shut, and dialled the number I knew best. When Fritz answered I told him I wanted to speak to Mr Wolfe.

'But Archie! He's at dinner!'

'I know. Tell him it's urgent.' That was another unexpected pleasure, having a good excuse to call Wolfe from the table. He has too many rules. His voice came, or rather his roar.

'Well?'

'I have a report. Saul and I are having an argument. He thought –'

'What the devil are you doing with Saul?'

'I'm telling you. He thought I should phone you. We have a problem of protocol. I tailed Byne to a restaurant, a joint, and Saul tailed Mrs Usher to the same restaurant, and our two subjects are in there together in a booth. Byne is eating oysters. So the question is, who is in charge, Saul or me? The only way to settle it without violence was to call you.'

'At meal time,' he said. I didn't retort, knowing that his complaint was not that I had presumed to interrupt, but that his two bright ideas had picked that moment to rendezvous.

I said sympathetically, 'They should have known better.'

'Is anyone with them?' he asked.

'No.'

'Do they know they have been seen?'

'No.'

'Could you eavesdrop?'

'Possibly, but I doubt it.'

'Very well, bring them. There's no hurry, since I have just started dinner. Give them no opportunity for a private exchange after they see you. Have you eaten?'

'I'm full of pie and milk. I don't know about Saul. I'll ask him.'

'Do so. He could come and eat – No. You may need him.'

I hung up, returned to our field headquarters, and told Saul, 'He wants them. Naturally. In an hour will do, since he just started dinner. Do you know what a genius is? A genius is a guy who makes things happen without his having any idea that they are going to happen. It's quite a trick. Our genius wanted to know if you've had anything to eat.'

'He would. Sure. Plenty.'

'Okay. Now the m.o. Do we take them in there or wait till they come out?'

Both procedures had pros and cons, and after discussion it was decided that Saul should go in and see how their meal was coming along, and when he thought they had swallowed enough to hold them through the hours ahead, or when they showed signs of adjourning, he would come out and wigwag me, go back in, and be near their booth when I approached.

They must have been fast eaters, for Saul hadn't been gone more than ten minutes when he came out, lifted a hand, saw me move, and went back in. I crossed over, entered, took five seconds to adjust to the noise and the smoke screen from the mob, made it to the rear, and there they were. The first Byne knew, someone was crowding him on the narrow seat, and his head jerked around. He started to say something, saw who it was, and goggled at me.

'Hi, Dinky,' I said. 'Excuse me for butting in, but I want to introduce a friend. Mr Panzer. Saul, Mrs Usher. Mr Byne. Sit down. Would you mind giving him room, Mrs Usher?'

Byne had started to rise, by reflex, but it can't be done in a tight little booth without toppling the table. He sank back. His mouth opened, and closed. Liquid spilled on the table top from a glass Elaine Usher was holding, and Saul, squeezed in beside her, reached and took it.

'Let me out,' Byne said. 'Let us out or I'll go out over you. Her name is Upson. Edith Upson.'

I shook my head. 'If you start a row you'll only make it worse. Mr Panzer knows Mrs Usher, though she doesn't know him. Let's be calm and consider the situation. There must be –'

'What do you want?'

'I'm trying to tell you. There must be some good reason why you two arranged to meet in this out-of-the-way dump, and Mr Panzer and I are curious to know what it is, and others will be too – the press, the public, the police, the District Attorney, and Nero Wolfe. I wouldn't expect you to explain it here in this din and smog. Either Mr Panzer can phone Inspector Cramer while I sit and chat with you, and he can send a car for you, or we'll take you to talk it over with Mr Wolfe, whichever you prefer.'

He had recovered some. He had played a lot of poker. He put a hand on my arm. 'Look, Archie, there's nothing to it. It looks funny, sure it does, us here together, but we didn't arrange it. I met Mrs Usher about a year ago, I went to see her when her daughter went to Grantham House, and when I came in here this evening and saw her, after what's happened, naturally I spoke to her and we –'

'Save it, Dinky. Saul, phone Cramer.'

Saul started to slide out. Byne reached and grabbed his sleeve. 'Now wait a minute. Damn it, can't you listen? I'm –'

'No,' I said. 'No listening. You can have one minute to decide.' I looked at my watch. 'In one minute either you and Mrs Usher come along to Nero Wolfe or we phone Cramer. One minute.' I looked at my watch. 'Go.'

'Not the cops,' Mrs Usher said. 'My God, not the cops.'

Byne began, 'If you'd only listen –'

'No. Forty seconds.'

If you're playing stud, and there's only one card to come, and the man across has two jacks showing and all you have is a mess, it doesn't matter what his hole card is, or yours either. Byne didn't use up the forty seconds. Only ten of them had gone when he stretched his neck to look for a waiter and ask for his check.

Chapter 13

Surveying Elaine Usher from my desk as she sat in the red leather chair, I told myself that Saul's picture of her, pieced together from a dozen descriptions he had got, had been pretty accurate. Oval face, blue eyes set close, good skin, medium-cut blonde hair, around forty. I would have said a hundred and fifteen pounds instead of a hundred and twenty, but she might have lost a few in the last four days. I had put her in the red leather chair because I had thought it desirable to have Byne closer to me. He was between Saul and me, and Saul was between the two subjects. But my arrangement was soon changed.

'I prefer,' Wolfe said, 'to speak with you separately, but first I must make sure that there is no misunderstanding. I intend to badger you, but you don't have to submit to it. Before I start, or at any moment, you may get up and leave. If you do, you will be through with me; thenceforth you will deal with the police. I make that clear because I don't want you bouncing up and down. If you want to go now, go.'

He took a deep breath. He had just come in from the dining-room, having had his coffee there while I reported on the summit conference at Tom's Joint.

'We were forced to come here by a threat,' Byne said.

'Certainly you were. And I am detaining you by the same threat. When you prefer that to this, leave. Now, madam, I wish to speak privately with Mr Byne. Saul, take Mrs Usher to the front room.'

'Don't go,' Byne told her. 'Stay here.'

Wolfe turned to me. 'You were right, Archie. He is incorrigible. It isn't worth it. Get Mr Cramer.'

'No,' Elaine Usher said. She left the chair. 'I'll go.'

Saul was up. 'This way,' he said, and went and opened the door to the front room and held it for her. When she had passed through he followed and closed the door.

Wolfe levelled his eyes at Byne. 'Now, sir. Don't bother to raise your voice; that wall and door are sound-proofed. Mr Goodwin has told me how you explained being in that restaurant with Mrs Usher. Do you expect me to accept it?'

'No,' Dinky said.

Of course. He had had time to realize that it wouldn't do. If he had gone to see her because her daughter was at Grantham House, how had he learned that she was Faith's mother? Not from the records and not from Mrs Irwin. From one of the other girls? It was too tricky.

'What do you substitute for it?' Wolfe asked.

'I told Goodwin that because the real explanation would have been embarrassing for Mrs Usher. Now I can't help it. I met her some time ago, three years ago, and for about a year I was intimate with her. She'll probably deny it. I'm pretty sure she will. Naturally she would.'

'No doubt. And your meeting her this evening was accidental?'

'No,' Dinky said. He had also had time to realize that that was too fishy. He went on, 'She phoned me this morning and said she was at the Christie Hotel, registered as Edith Upson. She had known that I was Mrs Robilotti's nephew, and she said she wanted to see me and ask me about her daughter who had died. I told her I hadn't been there Tuesday evening, and she said she knew that, but she wanted to see me. I agreed to see her because I didn't want to offend her. I didn't want it to get out that I had been intimate with Faith Usher's mother. We arranged to meet at that restaurant.'

'Had you known previously that she was Faith Usher's mother?'

'I had known that she had a daughter, but not that her name was Faith. She had spoken of her daughter when we – when I had known her.'

'What did she ask you about her daughter this evening?'

'She just wanted to know if I knew anything that hadn't been in the papers. Anything about the people there or exactly what had happened. I could tell her about the people, but I didn't know any more about what had happened than she did.'

'Do you wish to elaborate on any of this? Or add anything?'

'There's nothing to add.'

'Then I'll see Mrs Usher. After I speak with her I'll ask you in again, with her present. Archie, take Mr Byne and bring Mrs Usher.'

He came like a lamb. He had thrown away his discard and made his draw and his bets, and was ready for the show-down. I opened the door for him, held it for Mrs Usher to enter, closed it, and returned to my desk. She went to the red leather chair, so Wolfe had to swivel to face her. Another item of Saul's report on her had been that she liked men, and there were indications that men probably liked her – the way she handled her hips when she walked, the tilt of her head, the hint of a suggestion in her eyes, even now, when she was under pressure and when the man she was looking at was not a likely candidate for a frolic. And she was forty. At twenty she must have been a treat.

Wolfe breathed deep again. Exertion right after a meal was pretty rugged. 'Of course, madam,' he said, 'my reason for speaking with you and Mr Byne separately is transparent: to see if your account will agree with his. Since you have had no opportunity for collusion, agreement would be, if not conclusive, at least persuasive.'

She smiled. 'You use big words, don't you?' Something in her tone and her look conveyed the notion that for years she had been wanting to meet a man who used big words.

Wolfe grunted. 'I try to use words that say what I mean.'

'So do I,' she declared, 'but sometimes it's hard to find the ones I want. I don't know what Mr Byne told you, but all I can do is tell you the truth. You want to know how I happened to be with him there tonight, isn't that it?'

'That's it.'

'Well, I phoned him this morning and said I wanted to see him and he said he would meet me there at Tom's Joint, I had never heard of it before, at a quarter past seven. So I went. That's not very thrilling, is it?'

'Only moderately. Have you known him long?'

'I don't really *know* him at all. I met him somewhere about a year ago, and I wish I could tell you where, but I've been trying to remember and I simply *can't*. It was a party somewhere, but I can't remember where. Anyhow, it doesn't matter. But yesterday I was sitting at the window thinking about my daughter. My dear daughter Faith.' She stopped to gulp, but it wasn't very impressive. 'And I remembered meeting a man named Byne, Austin Byne, and someone telling me, maybe he told me himself, that he was the nephew of the rich Mrs Robilotti who used to be Mrs Albert Grantham. And my daughter had died at Mrs Robilotti's house, so maybe he could tell me about her, and maybe he could get Mrs Robilotti to see me so I could ask her about her. I wanted to learn all I could about my daughter.' She gulped.

It didn't look good. In fact, it looked bad. Byne had been smart enough to invent one that she couldn't be expected to corroborate; he had even warned that she would probably deny it; and what was worse, it was even possible that he hadn't invented it. He might have been telling the truth, like a gentleman. The meeting of Wolfe's two bright ideas at Tom's Joint, which had looked so rosy when Saul told me they were together, might fizzle out entirely. Maybe he wasn't a genius after all.

If he was sharing my gloom it didn't show. He asked, 'Since your rendezvous with Mr Byne was innocuous, why were you alarmed by his threat to call the police? What were her words, Archie?'

' "Not the cops. My God, not the cops." '

'Yes. Why, Mrs Usher?'

'I don't like cops. I never have liked cops.'

'Why did you leave your home and go to a hotel and register under another name?'

'Because of how I felt, what my daughter had done. I didn't want to see people. I knew newspapermen would come. And cops. I wanted to be alone. You would too if –'

The doorbell rang, and I went. Sometimes I let Fritz answer it when I am engaged, but with her there and Byne in the front room I thought I had better see who it was, and besides, I was having a come-down and felt like moving. It was only Orrie Cather. I opened up and greeted him, and he crossed the sill, and I shut the door. When he removed his coat there was disclosed a leather thing, a zippered case, that he had had under it.

'What's that?' I asked. 'Your week-end bag?'

'No,' he said. 'It's Mrs Usher's sec –'

My hand darted to clap on his mouth. He was startled, but he can take a hint, and when I headed down the hall and turned right to the dining-room he followed.

I shut the door, moved away from it, and demanded, 'Mrs Usher's what?'

'Her secret sin.' There was a gleam in his eye. 'I want to give it to Mr Wolfe myself.'

'You can't. Mrs Usher is in the office with him. Where did –'

'She's here? How come?'

'That can wait. Where did you get that thing?'

I may have sounded magisterial, but my nerves were a little raw. It put Orrie on his dignity. His chin went up. 'It's a pleasure to report, Mr Goodwin. Mr Panzer and I were covering the Christie Hotel. When the subject appeared and hopped a taxi he followed in one before I could join him. That left me loose and I phoned in. Mr Wolfe asked me if there had been any indication how long she would be gone, and I said yes, since she took a taxi it certainly wouldn't be less than half an hour and probably longer, and he said it would be desirable to take a look at her room, and I said fine. It took a while to get in. Do you want the details?'

'That can wait. What's in it?'

'It was in a locked suitcase – not the one the messenger took today, a smaller one. The suitcase was easy, but this thing had a trick lock and I had to bust it.'

I put out a hand. He hated to give it up, but protocol is protocol. I took it to the table, unzipped it, and pulled out two envelopes, one nine by twelve and the other one smaller. Neither was sealed, and hadn't been. I slipped out the contents of the big one.

They were pictures that had been clipped from magazines and newspapers. I would have recognized him even if there had been no captions, since I had been old enough to read for some years, and you often run across a picture of a multi-millionaire philanthropist. The one on top was captioned: 'Albert Grantham (left) receiving the annual award of the American Benevolent League.' They were all of Grantham, twenty or more. I started to turn them over, one by one, to see if anything was written on them.

'To hell with that,' Orrie said impatiently. 'It's the other one.'

It, not so big, held another envelope, smaller, of white rag bond. The engraved return in the corner said 'Albert Grantham,' with the Fifth Avenue address, and it was addressed in longhand to Mrs Elaine Usher, 812 West 87th Street, New York, and below was written 'By Messenger.' Inside were folded sheets. I unfolded them and read:

6 June 1952

My dear Elaine:

In accordance with my promise, I am confirming in writing what I said to you recently.

I am not accepting the obligations, legal or moral, of paternity of your daughter, Faith. You have always maintained that I am her father, and for a time I believed you, and I now have no evidence to prove you are wrong but, as I told you, I have taken the trouble to inform myself of your method of life for the past ten years, and it is quite clear that chastity is not one of your virtues. It may have been, during that period fifteen years ago when I took advantage of your youth and enjoyed your favours – you say it was – but your subsequent conduct makes it doubtful. I shall not again express my regret for my own conduct during that period. I have done that and you know how I feel about it, and have always felt since I achieved maturity, and I have not been illiberal in supplying the material needs of your daughter and yourself. For a time that was not easy, but since my father's death I have given you $2,000 each month, and you have paid no taxes on it.

But I am getting along in years, and you are quite right, I should make provision against contingencies. As I told you, I must reject your suggestion that I give you a large sum outright – large enough for you and your daughter to live on the income. I distrust your attitude towards money. I fear that in your hands the principal would soon be squandered, and you would again appeal to me. Nor can I provide for you through a trust fund, either now or in my will, for the reasons I gave you. I will not risk disclosure.

So I have taken steps that should meet the situation. I have given my nephew, Austin Byne, a portfolio of securities the income from which is tax exempt, amounting to slightly more than $2,000,000. The yield will be about $55,000 annually. My nephew is to remit half of it to you and keep the other half for himself.

This arrangement is recorded in an agreement signed by my nephew and myself. One provision is that if you make additional demands, if you disclose the relationship you and I once had, or if you make any claims on my estate or any member of my family, he is relieved of any obligation to share the income with you. Another provision is that if he fails to make the proper remittances to you with reasonable promptness you may claim the entire principal. In drafting that provision I would have liked to have legal advice, but could not. I am sure it is binding. I do not think my nephew will fail in his performance, but if he does you will know what to do. There is of course the possibility that *he* will squander the principal, but I have known him all his life and I am sure it is remote.

I have herewith kept my promise to confirm what I told you. I repeat that this letter is not to be taken as an acknowledgment by me that I am the father of your daughter, Faith. If you ever show it or use it as the basis of any claim, the remittances from my nephew will cease at once.

I close with all good wishes for the welfare and happiness of your daughter and yourself.

Yours sincerely,
Albert Grantham

As I finished and looked up Orrie said, 'I want to give it to Mr Wolfe myself.'

'I don't blame you.' I folded the sheets and put them in the envelope. 'Quite a letter. *Quite* a letter. I saw a note in the paper the other day that some bozo is doing a biography of him. He would love to have this. You lucky stiff. I'd give a month's pay for the kick you got when you found it.'

'It *was* nice. I want to give it to him.'

'You will. Wait here. Help yourself to champagne.'

I left, crossed to the office, stood until Wolfe finished a sentence, and told him, 'Mr Cather wants to show you something. He's in the dining-room.' He got up and went, and I sat down. Judging by the expression on Mrs Usher's face, she had been doing fine. I really would rather not have looked at her, to see the cocky little tilt of her head, the light of satisfaction in her eyes, knowing as I did that she was about to be hit by a ton of brick. So I didn't. I turned to my desk and opened a drawer and got out papers, and did things with them. When she told my back that she was glad I had brought them to Wolfe, she didn't mind a bit explaining to him, I wasn't even polite enough to turn around when I answered her. I had taken my notebook from my pocket and was tearing sketches of cats from it when Wolfe's footsteps came.

As he sat down he spoke. 'Bring Mr Byne, Archie. And Saul.'

I went and opened the door and said, 'Come in, gentlemen.'

As Byne entered his eyes went to Mrs Usher and saw what I had seen, and then he too was satisfied. They took the seats they had had before. Wolfe looked from one to the other and back again.

'I don't want to prolong this beyond necessity,' he said, 'but I would like to congratulate you. You were taken in that place by surprise and brought here with no chance to confer, but you have both lied so cleverly that it would have taken a long and costly investigation to impeach you. It was an admirable performance – If you please, Mr Byne. You may soon speak, and you will need to. Unfortunately, for you, the performance was wasted. Fresh ammunition has arrived. I have just finished reading a document that was not intended for me.' He looked at Mrs Usher. 'It states, madam, that if you disclose its contents you will suffer a severe penalty, but you have not disclosed them. On the contrary, you have done your best to safeguard them.'

Mrs Usher had sat up. 'What document? What are you talking about?'

'The best way to identify it is to quote an excerpt – say, the fourth paragraph. It goes: "So I have taken steps that should meet the situation. I have given my nephew, Austin Byne, a portfolio of securities the income from which is tax exempt, amounting to slightly more than $2,000,000. The yield will be about $55,000 annually. My nephew is to remit half." '

Byne was on his feet. The next few seconds were a little confused. I was up, to be between Byne and Wolfe, but the fury in his eyes was for Mrs Usher. Then, as he moved towards her, Saul was there to block him, so everything was under control. But then, with Saul's back to her and me cut off by Saul and Byne, Mrs Usher shot out of her chair and streaked for Wolfe. I might have beat her to it by diving across Wolfe's desk, but maybe not, from where I was, and anyway, I was too astonished to move – not by her, but by him. He had been facing her, so his knees weren't under the desk and he didn't have to swivel, but even so, he had a lot of pounds to get in motion. Back went his bulk, and up came his legs, and just as she arrived his feet were there, and one of them caught her smack on the chin. She staggered back into Saul's arms and he eased her on to the chair. And I'll be damned if she didn't put both hands to her jaw and squawk at Wolfe, 'You hit me!'

I had hold of Byne's arm, a good hold, and he didn't even know it. When he realized it he tried to jerk loose but couldn't, and for a second I thought he was going to swing with the other fist, and so did he.

'Take it easy,' I advised him. 'You're going to need all the breath you've got.'

'How did you get it?' Mrs Usher demanded. 'Where is it?' She was still clutching her jaw with both hands.

Wolfe was eyeing her, but not warily. Complacently, I would say. You might think that for a long time he had had a suppressed desire to kick a woman on the chin.

'It's in my pocket,' he said. He tapped his chest. 'I got it just now from the man who took it from your hotel room. You'll probably get it back in due course; that will depend; it may –'

'That's burglary,' Byne said. 'That's a felony.'

Wolfe nodded. 'By definition, yes. I doubt if Mrs Usher will care to make the charge if the document is eventually returned to her. It may be an exhibit in evidence in a murder trial. If so –'

'There has been no murder.'

'You are in error, Mr Byne. Will you please sit down? This will take a while. Thank you. I'll cover that point decisively with a categorical statement: Faith Usher was murdered.'

'No!' Mrs Usher said. Her hands left her jaw but remained poised, the fingers curved. 'Faith killed herself!'

'I'm not going to debate the point,' Wolfe told her. 'I say merely that I will stake my professional reputation on the statement that she was murdered – indeed, I have done so. That's why I am applying my resources and risking my credit. That's why I must explore the possibilities suggested by this letter.' He tapped his chest and focused on Byne. 'For instance, I shall insist on seeing the agreement between you and Mr Grantham. Does it provide that if Faith Usher should die your remittances to her mother are to be materially decreased, or even cease altogether?'

Byne wet his lips. 'Since you've read the letter to Mrs Usher you know what the agreement provides. It's a confidential agreement and you're not going to see it.'

'Oh, but I am.' Wolfe was assured. 'When you came here my threat was only to tell the police of your rendezvous. Now my threat is more imperative and may even be mortal. Observe Mrs Usher. Note her expression as she regards you. Have you seen the agreement, madam?'

'Yes,' she said, 'I have.'

'Does it contain such a provision as I suggested?'

'Yes,' she said, 'it does. It says that if Faith dies he can pay me only half as much or even less. Are you telling the truth, that she was murdered?'

'Nuts,' Byne said. 'It's not the truth he's after. Anyhow, I wasn't even there. Don't look at me, Elaine, look at *him*.'

'I thought,' Wolfe said, 'that it might save time to see the agreement now, so I sent Mr Cather to your apartment to look for it. It will expedite matters if you phone him and tell him where it is. He is good with locks and should be inside by this time.'

Byne was staring. 'By God,' he said.

'Do you want to phone him?'

'Not him. By God. You've been threatening to call the police. I'll call them myself. I'll tell them a man has broken into my apartment, and he's there now, and they'll get him.'

I left my chair. 'Here, Dinky, use my phone.'

He ignored me. 'It's not the agreement,' he told Wolfe. 'It's your goddamn nerve. He won't find the agreement because it's not there. It's in a safe-deposit box and it's going to stay there.'

'Then it must wait until Monday.' Wolfe's shoulders went up an eighth of an inch and down again. 'However, Mr Cather will not have his trouble for nothing. Aside from the chance that he may turn up other interesting items, he will use your typewriter, if you have one. I told him if he found one there to write something with it. I even told him what to write. This: "Have you found out yet that Edwin Laidlaw is the father of Faith Usher's baby? Ask him about his trip to Canada in August 1956." He will type that and bring it to me. You smile. You are amused? Because you don't have a typewriter?'

'Sure I have a typewriter. Did I smile?' He smiled again, a

poker smile. 'At you dragging Laidlaw in all of a sudden. I don't get it, but I suppose you do.'

'I didn't drag him in,' Wolfe asserted. 'Someone else did. The police received an unsigned typewritten communication which I have just quoted. And you were wrong to smile; that was a mistake. You couldn't possibly have been amused, so you must have been pleased, and by what? Not that you don't have a typewriter, because you have. I'll try a guess. Might it not have been that you were enjoying the idea of Mr Cather bringing me a sample of typing from your machine when you know it is innocent, and that you know it is innocent because you know where the guilty machine is? I think that deserves exploration. Unfortunately to-morrow is Sunday; it will have to wait. Monday morning Mr Goodwin, Mr Panzer, and Mr Cather will call at places where a machine might be easily and naturally available to you – for in-stance, your club. Another is the bank vault where you have a safe-deposit box. Archie. You go to my box regularly. Would it be remarkable for a vault customer to ask to use a typewriter?'

'Remarkable?' I shook my head. 'No.'

'Then that is one possibility. Actually,' he told Byne, 'I am not sorry that this must wait until Monday, for it does have a draw-back. The samples collected from the machines must be compared with the communication received by the police, and it is in their hands. I don't like that, but there's no other way. At least, if my guess is good, I will have exposed the sender of the communi-cation, and that will be helpful. On this point, sir, I do not threaten to go to the police; I am forced to.'

'You goddamn snoop,' Byne said through his teeth.

Wolfe's brows went up. 'I must have made a lucky guess. It's the machine at the vault?'

Byne's head jerked to Mrs Usher. 'Beat it, Elaine. I want to talk to him.'

Chapter 14

Austin Byne sat straight and stiff. When Saul had escorted Mrs Usher to the front room, staying there with her, I had told Dinky he would be more comfortable in the red leather chair, but from the way he looked at me I suspected that he had forgotten what 'comfortable' meant.

'You win,' he told Wolfe. 'So I spill my guts. Where do you want me to start?'

Wolfe was leaning back with his elbows on the chair arms and his palms together. 'First, let's clear up a point or two. Why did you send that thing about Laidlaw to the police?'

'I haven't said I sent it.'

'Pfui.' Wolfe was disgusted. 'Either you've submitted or you haven't. I don't intend to squeeze it out drop by drop. Why did you send it?'

Byne did have to squeeze it out. His lips didn't want to part. 'Because,' he finally managed, 'they were going on with the investigation and there was no telling what they might dig up. They might find out that I knew Faith's mother, and about my – about the arrangement. I still thought Faith had killed herself, and I still do, but if she *had* been murdered I thought Laidlaw must have done it and I wanted them to know about him and Faith.'

'Why must he have done it? You invented that, didn't you? About him and Miss Usher?'

'I did not. I sort of kept an eye on Faith, naturally. I don't mean I was with her, I just kept an eye on her. I saw her with Laidlaw twice, and the day he left for Canada I saw her in his car. I knew he went to Canada because a friend got a card from him. I didn't have to invent it.'

Wolfe grunted. 'You realize, Mr Byne, that everything you say is now suspect. Assuming that you knew that Laidlaw and Miss

Usher had in fact been intimate, why did you surmise that he had killed her? Was she menacing him?'

'Not that I know of. If he had a reason for killing her I didn't know what it was. But he was the only one of the people there that night who had had anything to do with her.'

'No. You had.'

'Damn it, I wasn't there!'

'That's true, but those who were there can also plead lack of opportunity. In the circumstances as I have heard them described, no one could have poisoned Miss Usher's champagne with any assurance that it would get to her. And you alone, of all those involved, had a motive, and not a puny one. An increase in annual income of $27,000 or more, tax exempt, is an alluring prospect. If I were you I would accept almost any alternative to a disclosure of that agreement to the District Attorney.'

'I am. I'm sitting here while you pile it on.'

'So you are.' Wolfe looked at his palms and put them on the chair arms. 'Now. Did you know that Miss Usher kept a bottle of poison on her person?'

No hesitation. 'I knew that she said she did. I never saw it. Her mother told me, and Mrs Irwin at Grantham House mentioned it to me once.'

'Did you know what kind of poison it was?'

'No.'

'Was it Mrs Usher's own idea to seclude herself in a hotel under another name, or did you suggest it?'

'Neither one. I mean I don't remember. She phoned me Thursday – no, Wednesday – and we decided she ought to do that. I don't remember who suggested it.'

'Who suggested your meeting this evening?'

'She did. She phoned me this morning. I told you that.'

'What did she want?'

'She wanted to know what I was going to do about payments, with Faith dead. She knew that by the agreement it was left to my discretion. I told her that for the present I would continue to send her half.'

'Had she been using any of the money you sent her to support her daughter?'

'I don't think so. Not for the last four or five years, but it wasn't her fault. Faith wouldn't take anything from her. Faith wouldn't live with her. They couldn't get along. Mrs Usher is very – unconventional. Faith left when she was sixteen, and for over a year we didn't know where she was. When I found her she was working in a restaurant. A waitress.'

'But you continued to pay Mrs Usher her full share?'

'Yes.'

'Is that fund in your possession and control without supervision?'

'Certainly.'

'It has never been audited?'

'Certainly not. Who would audit it?'

'I couldn't say. Would you object to an audit by an accountant of my selection? Now that I know of the agreement?'

'I certainly would. The fund is my property and I am accountable to no one but myself, as long as I pay Mrs Usher her share.'

'I must see that agreement.' Wolfe pursed his lips and slowly shook his head. 'It is extremely difficult,' he said, 'to circumvent the finality of death. Mr Grantham made a gallant try, but he was hobbled by his vain desire to guard his secret even after he became food for worms. He protected you and Mrs Usher, each against the frailty or knavery of the other, but what if you joined forces in a threat to his repute? He couldn't preclude that.' He lifted a hand to brush it aside. 'A desire to defeat death makes any man a fool. I must see that agreement. Meanwhile, a few points remain. You told Mr Goodwin that your selection of Miss Usher to be invited to that party was fortuitous, but now that won't do. Then why?'

'Of course,' Byne said. 'I knew that was coming.'

'Then you've had time to devise an answer.'

'I don't have to devise it. I was a damn fool. When I got the list from Mrs Irwin and saw Faith's name on it – well, there it was. The idea of having Faith as a guest at my aunt's house – it just appealed to me. Mrs Robilotti is only my aunt by marriage, you know. My mother was Albert Grantham's sister. You've got to admit there was a kick in the idea of having Faith sitting at my aunt's table. And then . . .'

He left it hanging. Wolfe prodded him. 'Then?'

'That suggested another idea, to have Laidlaw there too. I know I was a damn fool, but there it was. Laidlaw seeing Faith there, and Faith seeing him. Of course, my aunt could cross Faith off and tell Mrs Irwin – ' He stopped. In a second he went on, 'I mean you never knew what Faith would do, she might refuse to go, but Laidlaw wouldn't know she had been asked, so what the hell. So I suggested that to my aunt, to invite Laidlaw, and she did.'

'Did Miss Usher know that Albert Grantham had fathered her?'

'My God, no. She thought her father had been a man named Usher who had died before she was born.'

'Did she know you were the source of her mother's income?'

'No. I think – No, I don't think, I know. She suspected that her mother's income came from friends. From men she knew. That was why she left. About my picking Faith to be invited to that party and suggesting Laidlaw, after I had done that I got cold feet. I realized something might happen. At least Faith might walk out when she saw him, and it might be something worse, and I didn't want to be there, so I decided to get someone to go in my place. The first four or five I tried couldn't make it, and I thought of Archie Goodwin.'

Wolfe leaned back and closed his eyes, and his lips started to work. They pushed out and went back in, out and in, out and in ... Sooner or later he always does that, and I really should have a sign made, GENIUS AT WORK, and put it on his desk when he starts it. Usually I have some sort of idea as to what genius is working on, but that time not a glimmer. He had cleared away some underbrush, for instance who had sicked the cops on Laidlaw and how Faith and Laidlaw had both got invited to the party, but he had got only one thing to chew on, that he had at last found somebody who had had a healthy motive to kill Faith Usher, and Byne, as he liked to point out himself, hadn't even been at the party. Of course, that could have been what genius was at, doping out how Byne could have poisoned the champagne by remote control, but I doubted it.

Wolfe opened his eyes and aimed them at Dinky. 'I'm not going to wait until Monday,' he said. 'If I haven't enough now, I never will have. One thing you have told me, or at least implied, will have to be my peg. If I asked you about it now, you would only wriggle out with lies, so I won't bother. The time has come to attack the central question: if someone had decided to kill Faith Usher, how did he manage it?' He turned. 'Archie, get Mr Cramer.'

'No!' Byne was on his feet. 'Damn you, after I've spilled –'

I had lifted the receiver, but Byne was there, jostling and reaching. Wolfe's voice, with a snap, turned him. 'Mr Byne! Don't squeal until you're hurt. I've got you and I intend to keep you. Must I call Mr Panzer in?'

He didn't have to. Dinky backed away a step, giving me elbow room to dial, but close enough, he thought, to pounce. Getting Inspector Cramer at twenty minutes past ten on a Saturday evening can be anything from quick and simple to practically impossible. That time I had luck. He was at Homicide on Twentieth Street, and after a short wait I had him, and Wolfe got on, and Cramer greeted him with a growl, and Wolfe said he would need three minutes.

'I'll take all I can stand,' Cramer said. 'What is it?'

'About Faith Usher. I am being pestered beyond endurance. Take yesterday. In the morning those four men insisted on seeing me. In the afternoon you barged in. In the evening Mr Goodwin and I were interrupted by a phone call summoning him to Mrs Robilotti's house, and when he goes he finds Mr Skinner there, and he –'

'Do you mean the Commissioner?'

'Yes. He said it was unofficial and off the record, and made an offensive proposal which Mr Goodwin was to refer to me. I don't complain of that to you, since he is your superior and you presumably didn't know about it.'

'I didn't.'

'But it was another thorn for me, and I have had enough. I would like to put an end to it. All this hullabaloo has been caused by Mr Goodwin's conviction, as an eye-witness, that Faith Usher did not kill herself, and I intend to satisfy myself on the point independently. If I decide he is wrong I will deal with him. If I decide he is right it will be because I will have uncovered evidence that may have escaped you. I notify you of my intention because in order to proceed I must see all of the people involved, I must invite them to my office, and I thought you should know about it.

Also I thought you might choose to be present, and if so you will be welcome, but in that case you should get them here. I will not ask people to my office for a conference and then confront them with a police inspector. Tomorrow morning at eleven o'clock would be a good time.'

Cramer made a noise, something like 'Wmgzwmzg'. Then he found words. 'So you've got your teeth in something. What?'

'It's other people's teeth that are in something. In me. And I'm annoyed. The situation is precisely as I have described it and I have nothing to add.'

'You wouldn't have. Tomorrow is Sunday.'

'Yes. Since three of them are girls with jobs that is just as well.'

'You want all of them?'

'Yes.'

'Are any of them with you now?'

'No.'

'Is Commissioner Skinner in this?'

'No.'

'I'll call you back in an hour.'

'That won't do,' Wolfe objected. 'If I am to invite them I must start at once, and it's late.'

Not only that, but he knew darned well that if he gave him an hour Cramer would probably ring our bell in about ten minutes and want in. Anyway, it was a cinch that Cramer would buy it, and after a few more foolish questions he did.

We hung up, and Wolfe turned to Byne, who had returned to his chair. 'Now for you,' he said, 'and Mrs Usher. I do not intend to let you communicate with anyone, and there is only one way to insure against it. She will spend the night here; there is a spare room with a good bed. It is a male household, but that shouldn't disconcert her. There is another room you may use, or, if you prefer, Mr Panzer will accompany you home and sleep there, and bring you here in the morning. Mr Cramer will have the others here at eleven o'clock.'

'You can go to hell,' Byne said. He stood up. 'I'm taking Mrs Usher to her hotel.'

Wolfe shook his head. 'I know your mind is in disorder, but surely you must see that that is out of the question. I can't possibly allow you an opportunity to repair any of the gaps I have made in your fences. If you scoot I shall move at once, and you'll find you have no fences left at all. Only by my sufferance can you hope to get out of this mess without disfigurement, and you know it. Archie, bring Saul and Mrs Usher – no. First ring Mr Byne's apartment and tell Orrie to come. Also tell him not to be disappointed at not finding the agreement; it isn't there. If he has found any items that seem significant he might as well bring them.'

'You goddamn snoop,' Dinky said, merely repeating himself.

I turned to the phone.

Chapter 15

For an hour and a half Sunday morning Fritz and I worked like beavers, setting the stage. The idea was – that is, Wolfe's idea – to reproduce as nearly as possibly the scene of the crime, and it was a damn silly idea, since you could have put seven or eight of that office into Mrs Robilotti's drawing-room. Taking the globe and the couch and the television cabinet and a few other items to the dining-room helped a little, but it was still hopeless. I wanted to go up to the plant rooms and tell Wolfe so, and add that if a play-back was essential to his programme he had better break his rule never to leave the house on business and move the whole per-formance uptown to Mrs Robilotti's, but Fritz talked me out of it. To get fourteen chairs we had to bring some down from upstairs, and then it developed later that some of them weren't really necessary. The bar was a table over in the far corner, but it couldn't be against the wall because there had to be room for Hackett behind it. One small satisfaction I got was that the red leather chair had been taken to the dining-room with the other stuff, and Cramer wouldn't like that a bit.

Furniture-moving wasn't all. Mrs Usher kept buzzing on the house phone from the South Room, for more coffee, for more towels, though she had a full supply, for a section she said was missing from the Sunday paper I had taken her, and for an ad-ditional list of items I had to get from the drugstore. Then at ten-fifteen here came Austin Byne, escorted by Saul, demanding a private audience with Wolfe immediately, and to get him off my neck I had Saul take him up the three flights to the vestibule of the plant rooms, where they found the door locked, and then Saul had to get physical with him when he wanted to open doors on the upper floors trying to find Mrs Usher.

I expected more turmoil when, at ten-forty, the bell rang and

Inspector Cramer was on the stoop, but it wasn't Wolfe he had come early for. He merely asked if Mrs Robilotti had arrived, and, when I told him no, stayed outside. Theoretically, in a democracy, a police inspector should react just the same to a dame with a Fifth Avenue mansion as to an unmarried mother, but a job is a job, and facts are facts and one fact was that the Commissioner himself had taken the trouble to make a trip to the mansion. So I didn't chalk it up against Cramer that he waited out on the sidewalk for the Robilotti limousine; and anyway, he was there to greet the three unmarried mothers when Sergeant Purley Stebbins arrived with them in a police car. The three chevaliers, Paul Schuster, Beverly Kent, and Edwin Laidlaw, came singly, on their own.

I had promised myself a certain pleasure, and I didn't let Cramer's one-man reception committee interfere with it. When the limousine finally rolled to the curb, a few minutes late, and he convoyed Mrs Robilotti up the stoop steps, followed by her husband, son, daughter, and butler, I held the door for them as they entered and then left them to Fritz. My objective was the last one in, Hackett. When he had crossed the sill I put my hands ready for his coat and hat, in the proper manner exactly.

'Good morning, sir,' I said. 'A pleasant day. Mr Wolfe will be down shortly.'

It got him. He darted a glance at the others, saw that no eye was on him, handed me his hat, and said, 'Quite. Thank you, Goodwin.'

That made the day for me personally, no matter how it turned out professionally. I took him to the office and then went to the kitchen, buzzed the plant rooms on the house phone, and told Wolfe the cast had arrived.

'Mrs Usher?' he asked.

'Okay. In her room. She'll stay put.'

'Mr Byne?'

'Also okay. In the office with the others, with Saul glued to him.'

'Very well. I'll be down.'

I went and joined the mob. They were scattered around, some seated and some standing. I permitted myself a private grin when I saw that Cramer, finding the red leather chair gone, had moved one of the yellow ones to its exact position and put Mrs Robilotti in it, and was on his feet beside it, bending down to her. As I threaded my way through to my desk the sound of the elevator came, and in a moment Wolfe entered.

No pronouncing of names was required, since he had met the Robilottis and the Grantham twins at the time of the jewellery hunt. He made it to his desk, sent his eyes around, and sat. He looked at Cramer.

'You have explained the purpose of this gathering, Mr Cramer?'

'Yes. You're going to prove that Goodwin is either wrong or right.'

'I didn't say "prove". I said I intend to satisfy myself and deal with him accordingly.' He surveyed the audience. 'Ladies and gentlemen. I will not keep you long – at least, not most of you. I have no exhortation for you and no questions to ask. To form an opinion of Mr Goodwin's competence as an eye-witness, I need to see, not what he saw, since these quarters are too cramped for that, but an approximation of it. You cannot take your positions precisely as they were last Tuesday evening, or re-enact the scene with complete fidelity, but we'll do the best we can. Archie?'

I left my chair to stage-manage. Thinking that Mrs Robilotti and her Robert were the most likely to baulk, I left them till the last. First I put Hackett behind the table, which was the bar, and Laidlaw and Helen Yarmis at one end of it. Then Rose Tuttle and Beverly Kent, on chairs over where the globe had stood. Then Celia Grantham and Paul Schuster by the wall to the right of Wolfe's desk, with her sitting and him standing. Then I put Saul Panzer on a chair near the door to the hall, and told the audience, 'Mr Panzer here is Faith Usher. The distance is wrong and so are the others, but the relative positions are about right.' Then I put an ashtray on a chair to the right of the safe, and told them, 'This is Faith Usher's bag, containing the bottle of poison.' With all that arranged, I didn't think Mrs Robilotti would protest when I asked her and her husband to take their places in front of the bar, and she didn't.

That was all, except for Ethel Varr and me, and I got her and stood with her at a corner of my desk, and told Wolfe, 'All set.'

'Miss Tuttle and I were much farther away,' Beverly Kent objected.

'Yes, sir,' Wolfe agreed. 'It is not presumed that this is identical. Now.' His eyes went to the group at the bar. 'Mr Hackett, I understand that when Mr Grantham went to the bar for champagne for himself and Miss Usher, two glasses were there in readiness. You had poured one of them a few minutes previously, and the other just before he arrived. Is that correct?'

'Yes, sir.' Hackett had fully recovered from our brush in the hall and was back in character. 'I have stated to the police that one of the glasses had been standing there three or four minutes.'

'Please pour a glass now and put it in place.'

The bottles in the cooler on the table were champagne, and good champagne; Wolfe had insisted on it. Fritz had opened two of them. Pouring champagne is always nice to watch, but I doubt if any pourer ever had as attentive an audience as Hackett had, as he took a bottle from the cooler and filled a glass.

'Keep the bottle in your hand,' Wolfe directed him. 'I'll explain what I'm after and then you may proceed. I want to see it from various angles. You will pour another glass, and Mr Grantham will come and get the two glasses and go with them to Mr Panzer – that is to say, to Miss Usher. He will hand him one, and Mr Goodwin will be there and take the other one. Meanwhile you will be pouring two more glasses, and Mr Grantham will come and get them and go with them to Miss Tuttle, and hand her one, and again Mr Goodwin will be there and take the other one. You will do the same with Miss Varr and Miss Grantham. Not with Miss Yarmis and Mrs Robilotti, since they are there at the bar. That way I shall see it from all sides. Is that clear, Mr Hackett?'

'Yes, sir.'

'It's not clear to me,' Cecil said. 'What's the idea? I didn't do that. All I did was get two glasses and take one to Miss Usher.'

'I'm aware of that,' Wolfe told him. 'As I said, I want to get various angles on it. If you prefer, Mr Panzer can move to the different positions, but this is simpler. I only request your co-operation. Do you find my request unreasonable?'

'I find it pretty damn nutty. But it's all nutty, in my opinion, so a little more won't hurt, if I can keep a glass for myself when I've performed.' He moved, then turned. 'What's the order again?'

'The order is unimportant. After Mr Panzer, Misses Tuttle, Varr, and Grantham, in any order you please.'

'Right. Start pouring, Hackett. Here I come.'

The show started. It did seem fairly nutty, at that, especially my part. Hackett pouring, and Cecil carrying, and the girls taking – there was nothing odd about that; but me racing around, taking the second glass, deciding what to do with it, doing it, and getting to the next one in time to be there waiting when Cecil arrived – of all the miscellaneous chores I had performed at Wolfe's direction over the years, that took the prize. At the fourth and last one, for Celia Grantham, by the wall to the right of Wolfe's desk, Cecil cheated. After he had handed his sister hers he ignored my out-stretched hand, raised his glass, said, 'Here's to crime,' and took a mouthful of the bubbles. He lowered the glass and told Wolfe, 'I hope that didn't spoil it.'

'It was in bad taste,' Celia said.

'I meant it to be,' he retorted. 'This whole thing has been in bad taste from the beginning.'

Wolfe, who had straightened up to watch the performance, let his shoulders down. 'You didn't spoil it,' he said. His eyes went around. 'I invite comment. Did anyone notice anything worthy of remark?'

'I don't know whether it's worthy of remark or not,' Paul Schuster, the lawyer, said, 'but this exhibition can't possibly be made the basis for any conclusion. The conditions were not the same at all.'

'I must disagree,' Wolfe disagreed. 'I did get a basis for a conclusion, and for the specific conclusion I had hoped for. I need support for it, but would rather not suggest it. I appeal to all of you: did anything about Mr Grantham's performance strike your eye?'

A growl came from the door to the hall. Sergeant Purley Stebbins was standing there on the sill, his big frame half filling the rectangle. 'I don't know about a conclusion,' he said, 'but I noticed that he carried the glasses the same every time. The one in his right hand, his thumb and two fingers were on the bowl and the one in his left hand, he held that lower down, by the stem. And he kept the one in his right hand and handed them the one in his left hand. Every time.'

I had never before seen Wolfe look at Purley with unqualified admiration. 'Thank you, Mr Stebbins,' he said. 'You not only have eyes but know what they're for. Will anyone corroborate him?'

'I will,' Saul Panzer said. 'I do.' He was still holding the glass Cecil had handed him.

'Will you, Mr Cramer?'

'I reserve it.' Cramer's eyes were narrowed at him. 'What's your conclusion?'

'Surely that's obvious.' Wolfe turned a hand over. 'What I hoped to get was ground for a conclusion that anyone who was sufficiently familiar with Mr Grantham's habits, and who saw him pick up the glasses and start off with them, would know which one he would hand to Miss Usher. And I got it, and I have two competent witnesses, Mr Stebbins and Mr Panzer.' His head turned. 'That is all, ladies and gentlemen. I wish to continue, but only to Mrs Robilotti, Mr Byne, and Mr Laidlaw – and Mr Robilotti by courtesy, if he chooses to stay. The rest of you may go. I needed your help for this demonstration and I thank you for coming. It would be a pleasure to serve you champagne on some happier occasion.'

'You mean we have to go?' Rose Tuttle piped. 'I want to stay.'

Judging from the expressions on most of the faces, the others did too, except Helen Yarmis, who was standing by the bar with Laidlaw. She said, 'Come on, Ethel,' to Ethel Varr, who was standing by my desk, and they headed for the door. Cecil emptied his glass and put it on Wolfe's desk and announced that he was staying, and Celia said she was too. Beverly Kent, the diplomat, showed that he had picked the right career by handling Rose Tuttle, who was seated beside him. She let him escort her out. Paul Schuster approached to listen a moment to the twins arguing with Wolfe, and then turned and went. Seeing Cramer cross to Mrs Robilotti, at the bar with her husband, I noted that Hackett wasn't there and then found that he wasn't anywhere. He had gone without my knowing it, one more proof that a detective is no match for a butler.

It was Mrs Robilotti who settled the issue with the twins. She came to Wolfe's desk, followed by Cramer and her husband, and told them to go, and then turned to her husband and told him to go too. Her pale grey eyes, back under her angled brows, were little circles of tinted ice. It was Celia she looked at.

'This man needs a lesson,' she said, 'and I'll give it to him. I never have needed you, and I don't need you now. You're being absurd. I do things better alone, and I'll do this alone.'

Celia opened her mouth, closed it again, turned to look at Laidlaw, and went, and Cecil followed. Robilotti started to speak, met the pale grey eyes, shrugged like a polished and civilized Italian, and quit. When her eyes had seen him to the door, she walked to the chair Cramer had placed for her when she arrived, sat, aimed the eyes at Wolfe, and spoke.

'You said you wished to continue. Well?'

He was polite. 'In a moment, madam. Another person is expected. If you gentlemen will be seated? Archie?'

Saul was already seated, still in Faith Usher's place, sipping champagne. Leaving it to the other four, Laidlaw, Byne, Cramer, and Stebbins to do their own seating, I went to the hall, mounted the two flights to the South Room, knocked on the door, was told to come in, and did so.

Elaine Usher, in a chair by a window with sections of the Sunday paper scattered on the floor, had a mean look ready for me.

'Okay,' I said. 'Your cue.'

'It's about time.' She kicked the papers away from her feet and got up. 'Who's there?'

'As expected. Mr Wolfe. Byne, Laidlaw, Panzer. Inspector Cramer and Sergeant Stebbins. Mrs Robilotti. She sent her husband home. I take you straight to her.'

'I know. I'll enjoy that, I really will, no matter what happens. My hair's a mess. I'll be with you in a minute.'

She went to the bathroom and closed the door. I wasn't impatient, since Wolfe would use the time to get Mrs Robilotti into a proper mood. Mrs Usher used it too. When she emerged her hair was very nice and her lips were the colour that excites a bull. I asked her if she preferred the elevator, and she said no, and I followed her down the two flights. As we entered the office I was at her elbow.

It came out so perfect that you might have thought it had been rehearsed. I crossed with her, passing between Cramer and Byne, turned so we were facing Mrs Robilotti, right in front of her, and said, 'Mrs Robilotti, let me present Mrs Usher, the mother of Faith Usher.' Mrs Usher bent at the waist, put out a hand, and said, 'It's a pleasure, a great pleasure.' Mrs Robilotti stared a second, shot a hand out, and slapped Mrs Usher's face. Perfect.

Chapter 16

Your guess is as good as mine, whether Wolfe would have been able to crash through anyway if the confrontation stunt hadn't worked – if Mrs Robilotti had been quick enough and tough enough to take Mrs Usher's offered hand and respond according to protocol. He maintains that he would have, but that the question is academic, since with Mrs Robilotti's nerves already on edge the sudden appearance of that woman, without warning, bending to her and offering a hand, was sure to break her.

I didn't pull Mrs Usher back in time to dodge the slap, though I might have, but after it landed I acted. After all she was a house guest, and a kick on the chin by the host and a smack in the face by another guest were no credit to our hospitality; and besides, she might try to return the compliment. So I gripped her arm and pulled her back out of range, bumping into Cramer, who had bounced out of his chair. Mrs Robilotti had jerked back and sat stiff, her teeth pinning her lower lip.

'It might be well,' Wolfe told me, 'to seat Mrs Usher near you. Madam, I regret the indignity you have suffered under my roof.' He gestured. 'That is Mr Laidlaw. Mr Cramer, of the police. Mr Stebbins, also of the police. You know Mr Byne.'

As I was convoying her to the chair Saul had brought, putting her between Laidlaw and me, Cramer was saying, 'You stage it and then you regret it.' To his right: 'I do regret it, Mrs Robilotti. I had no hand in it.' Back to Wolfe: 'All right, let's hear it.'

'You have seen it,' Wolfe told him. 'Certainly I staged it. You heard me deliberately bait Mrs Robilotti, to ensure the desired reaction to Mrs Usher's appearance. Before commenting on that reaction, I must explain Mr Laidlaw's presence. I asked him to stay because he has a legitimate concern. As you know, someone sent an anonymous communication making certain statements about him, and that entitles him to hear disclosure of the truth. Why Mr Byne is here will soon be apparent. It was something he said last evening that informed me that Mrs Robilotti had known that her former husband, Albert Grantham, was the father of Faith Usher. However –'

'That's a lie,' Byne said. 'That's a damn lie.'

Wolfe's tone sharpened. 'I choose my words, Mr Byne. I didn't say you told me that, but that something you said informed me. Speaking of the people invited to that gathering, you said, "Of course, my aunt could cross Faith off and tell Mrs Irwin" – and stopped, realizing that you had slipped. When I let it pass, you thought I had missed it, but I hadn't. It was merely that if I had tried to pin you down you would have wriggled out by denying the implication. Now that –'

'There was no implication!'

'Nonsense. Why should your aunt "cross Faith off"? Why should she refuse to have Miss Usher in her house? Granting that there were many possible explanations, there was one suggested by the known facts: that she would not receive as a guest the natural daughter of her former husband. And I had just learned that Faith Usher was Albert Grantham's natural daughter, and that you were aware of it. So I had the implication, and I arranged to test it. If Mrs Robilotti, suddenly confronted by Faith Usher's mother extending a friendly hand, took the hand and betrayed no reluctance, the implication would be discredited. I expected her to shrink from it, and I was wrong. I may learn some day that what a woman will do is beyond conjecture. Instead of shrinking, she struck. I repeat, Mrs Usher, I regret it. I did not foresee it.'

'You can't have it both ways,' Byne said. 'You say my aunt wouldn't have Faith Usher in her house because she knew she was her former husband's natural daughter. But she did have her in her house. She knew she had been invited, and she let her come.'

Wolfe nodded. 'I know. That's the point. That's my main reason for assuming that your aunt killed her. There are other –'

'Hold it,' Cramer snapped. His head turned. 'Mrs Robilotti, I want you to know that this is as shocking to me as it is to you.'

Her pale grey eyes were on Wolfe and she didn't move them.

152

'I doubt it,' she said. 'I didn't know any man could go as low as *this*. This is incredible.'

'I agree,' Wolfe told her. 'Murder is always incredible. I have now committed myself, madam, before witnesses, and if I am wrong I shall be at your mercy. I wouldn't like that. Mr Cramer. You are shocked. I can expound, or you can attack. Which do you prefer?'

'Neither one.' Cramer's fists were on his knees. 'I just want to know. What evidence have you that Faith Usher was Albert Grantham's daughter?'

'Well.' Wolfe cocked his head. 'That is a ticklish point. My sole concern in this is the murder of Faith Usher, and I have no desire to make unnecessary trouble for people not implicated in it. For example, I know where you can find evidence that the death of Faith Usher meant substantial financial profit for a certain man, but since he wasn't there and couldn't have killed her, I'll tell you about it only if it becomes requisite. To answer your question: I have statements of two people, Mrs Elaine Usher and Mr Austin Byne.' His eyes moved. 'And, Mr Byne, you have trimmed long enough. Did your aunt know that Faith Usher was the daughter of Albert Grantham?'

Dinky's jaw worked. He looked left, at Mrs Usher, but not right, at his aunt. Wolfe had made it plain: if he came through, Wolfe would not tell Cramer about the agreement and where it was. Probably what decided him was the fact that Mrs Robilotti had already given it away by slapping Mrs Usher.

'Yes,' he said. 'I told her.'

'When?'

'A couple of months ago.'

'Why?'

'Because – something she said. She had said it before, that I was a parasite because I was living on money my uncle had given me before he died. When she said it again that day I lost my temper and told her that my uncle had given me the money so I could provide for his illegitimate daughter. She wouldn't believe me, and I told her the name of the daughter and her mother. Afterwards I was sorry I had told her, and I told her so –'

A noise, an explosive noise, came from his aunt. 'You liar,' she said, a glint of hate in the pale grey eyes. 'You sit there and lie. You told me so you could blackmail me, to get more millions out of me. The millions Albert had given you weren't enough. You weren't satisfied –'

'Stop it!' Wolfe's voice was a whip. He was scowling at her. 'You are in mortal peril, madam. I have put you there, so I have a responsibility, and I advise you to hold your tongue. Mr Cramer. Do you want more from Mr Byne, or more from me?'

'You.' Cramer was so shocked he was hoarse. 'You say that Mrs Robilotti deliberately let Faith Usher come to that party so she could kill her. Is that right?'

'Yes.'

'And that her motive was that she knew that Faith Usher was the illegitimate child of Albert Grantham?'

'It could have been. With her character and temperament that could have been sufficient motive. But she has herself just suggested an additional one. Her nephew may have been using Faith Usher as a fulcrum to pry a fortune out of her. You will explore that.'

'I certainly will. That show you put on. You say that proved that Mrs Robilotti could have done it?'

'Yes. You saw it. She could have dropped the poison into the glass that had been standing there for three or four minutes. She stayed there at the bar. If someone else had started to take that glass she could have said it was hers. When her son came and picked up the two glasses, if he had taken the poisoned one in his right hand, which would have meant – to her, since she knew his habits – that he would drink it himself, again she could have said it was hers and told him to get another one. Or she could even have handed it to him, have seen to it that he took the poisoned one in his left hand; but you can't hope to establish that, since neither she nor her son would admit it. The moment he left the bar with the poisoned glass in his left hand Faith Usher was doomed; and the risk was slight, since an ample supply of cyanide was there on a chair in Miss Usher's bag. It would unquestionably be assumed that she had committed suicide; indeed, it was assumed, and the assumption would have prevailed if Mr Goodwin hadn't been there and kept his eyes open.'

'Who told Mrs Robilotti that Miss Usher had the poison? And when?'

'I don't know.' Wolfe gestured. 'Confound it, must I shine your shoes for you?'

'No, I'll manage. You've shined enough. You say the risk was slight. It wasn't slight when she got Miss Usher's bag and took out the bottle and took some of the poison.'

'I doubt if she did that. I doubt if she ever went near that bag. If she knew that the poison Miss Usher carried around was cyanide, and several people did, she probably got some somewhere else, which isn't difficult, and had it at hand. I suggest that that is worth inquiry, whether she recently had access to a supply of cyanide. You might even find that she had actually procured some.' Wolfe gestured again. 'I do not pretend that I am showing you a ripened fruit which you need only to pick. I undertook merely to satisfy myself whether Mr Goodwin was right or wrong. I am satisfied. Are you?'

Cramer never said. Mrs Robilotti was on her feet. I had the idea then that what moved her was Wolfe's mentioning the possibility that she had got hold of cyanide somewhere else, and learned a few days later that I had been right, when Purley Stebbins told me that they had found out where she got it, and could prove it. Anyhow, she was on her feet, and moving, but had taken only three steps when she had to stop. Cramer and Purley were both there blocking the way, and together they weigh four hundred pounds and are over four feet wide.

'Let me pass,' she said. 'I'm going home.'

I have seldom felt sorry for that pair, but I did then, especially Cramer.

'Not right now,' he said gruffly. 'I'm afraid you'll have to answer some questions.'

Chapter 17

One item. You may remember my mentioning that one day, the day after the murderer of Faith Usher was convicted, I was discussing with a friend what was the most conceited remark we had ever heard? It was that same day that I caught sight of Edwin Laidlaw in the men's bar at the Churchill and decided to do a good deed. Besides, I had felt that the amount on the bill we had sent him, which he had paid promptly without a murmur, had been pretty stiff, and he had something coming. So I approached him, and after greetings had been exchanged I performed the deed.

'I didn't want to mention it,' I said, 'while her mother was on trial for murder, but now I can tell you, in case you're interested. One day during that commotion I was talking with Celia Grantham, and your name came up, and she said, "I may marry him some day. If he gets into a bad jam I'll marry him now." I report it only because I thought you might want to take some dancing lessons.'

'I don't have to,' he said. 'I appreciate it, and many thanks, but we're getting married next week. On the quiet. We put it off until the trial was over. Let me buy you a drink.'

There you are. I'm one good deed shy.

813.52 STO

STO Stout, Rex
     Champagne for one.

DATE DUE			
6/26/01			

LIBRARY
SAINT MARY'S CONVENT
NOTRE DAME, INDIANA

Scribners